"Flora, you remember Conner?"

It didn't matter how many rules or hearts he'd broken, there wasn't a woman alive who could forget Conner MacNeil once she'd met him.

Determined not to boost his ego by revealing her thoughts, Flora adopted what she hoped was a puzzled expression. "Conner—Conner—the name *is* familiar. Were you below me at school? Or were you above me?"

His blue eyes glinted with wicked humor. "I don't recall ever being above or below you, Flora," he murmured softly.

She felt the heat flare in her cheeks and remembered, too late, that anyone trying to play word games with Conner was always going to lose.

Flora didn't know why she felt so hot and bothered. The only person who didn't seem remotely embarrassed was Conner himself. He simply laughed.

Flora bit her lip. She knew she ought to say something nice and welcoming, but her brain just didn't seem to be working with its normal efficiency. Seeing Conner again without warning was shocking, confusing and...*thrilling?*

One thing she knew for sure—the calm, tranquil routine of Glenmore Island was about to be overturned.

Dear Reader,

On the surface, Conner MacNeil is the ultimate bad boy. He had a rough start in life and was always in trouble. When he finally turned his back on Glenmore, the islanders were as pleased to see him go as he was to leave.

Now he's back, and the boy is now a man. He's also a doctor, and his arrival sends the traditional, close-knit community of Glenmore into an uproar. Islanders have long memories, and they find it hard to believe that wild, unstable Conner is capable of fulfilling such a responsible role.

Only the practice nurse, Flora Harris, is willing to give Conner the benefit of the doubt. She has been fascinated by Conner since childhood, and she soon finds her feelings for him growing into something deeper and more permanent.

But their differences soon make the relationship complicated. Flora is a very private person. She hates being talked about—and everyone is talking about Conner. *He* doesn't care, but she certainly does. This is her home, and she doesn't want people gossiping. So she and Conner try and keep their relationship private, forgetting that on an island like Glenmore, nothing remains a secret for long....

Will the islanders finally learn to trust their new doctor? Will Conner and Flora's relationship survive the pressure of public scrutiny?

I hope you enjoy reading Conner and Flora's story, set on the wild, wind-battered shores of Glenmore Island.

Love,

Sarah

THE REBEL DOCTOR'S BRIDE
Sarah Morgan

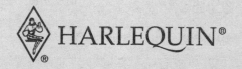

HARLEQUIN®

TORONTO • NEW YORK • LONDON
AMSTERDAM • PARIS • SYDNEY • HAMBURG
STOCKHOLM • ATHENS • TOKYO • MILAN • MADRID
PRAGUE • WARSAW • BUDAPEST • AUCKLAND

ISBN-13: 978-0-373-19919-8
ISBN-10:   0-373-19919-8

THE REBEL DOCTOR'S BRIDE

First North American Publication 2008

www.eHarlequin.com

Printed in U.S.A.

THE REBEL DOCTOR'S BRIDE

PROLOGUE

THEY were all staring.

He could feel them staring even though he stood with his back to them, his legs braced against the slight roll of the ferry, his eyes fixed firmly on the ragged coastline of the approaching island.

The whispers and speculation had started from the moment he'd ridden his motorbike onto the ferry. *From the moment he'd removed his helmet and allowed them to see his face.*

Some of the passengers were tourists, using the ferry as a means to spend a few days or weeks on the wild Scottish island of Glenmore, but many were locals, taking advantage of their only transport link with the mainland.

And the locals knew him. Even after an absence of twelve years, they recognised him.

They remembered him for all the same reasons that he remembered them.

Their faces were filed away in his subconscious; deep scars on his soul.

He probably should have greeted them; islanders were sociable people and a smile and a 'hello' might have begun to bridge the gulf that stretched between them. But his firm mouth didn't shift and the chill in his ice blue eyes didn't thaw.

And that was the root of the problem, he brooded silently as he studied the deadly rocks that had protected this part of the coastline for centuries. He wasn't sociable. He didn't care what they thought of him. He'd never been interested in courting the good opinion of others and he'd never considered himself an islander, even though he'd been born on Glenmore and had spent the first eighteen years of his life trapped within the confines of its rocky shores.

He had no wish to exchange small talk or make friends. Neither did he intend to explain his presence. They'd find out what he was doing here soon enough. It was inevitable. But, for now, he dismissed their shocked glances as inconsequential and enjoyed his last moments of self-imposed isolation.

The first drops of rain sent the other passengers scuttling inside for protection but he didn't move. Instead he stood still, staring bleakly at the ragged shores of the island, just visible through the rain-lashed mist. The land was steeped in lore and legend, with a long, bloody history of Viking invasion.

Locals believed that the island had a soul and a personality. They believed that the unpredictable weather was Glenmore expressing her many moods.

He glanced up at the angry sky with a cynical smile. If that was the case then today she was definitely menopausal.

Or maybe, like the islanders, she'd seen his return and was crying.

The island loomed out of the mist and he stared ahead, seeing dark memories waiting on the shore. *Memories of wild teenage years; of anger and defiance.* His past was a stormy canvas of rules broken, boundaries exploded, vices explored, girls seduced—*far too many girls seduced*—and all against an atmosphere of intense disapproval from the locals who'd thought his parents should have had more control.

Remembering the vicious, violent atmosphere of his home, he gave a humourless laugh. His father hadn't been capable of controlling himself, let alone him. After his mother had left, he'd spent as little time in the house as possible.

The rain was falling heavily as the ferry docked and he

turned up the collar of his leather jacket and moved purpose-fully towards his motorbike.

He could have replaced his helmet and assured himself a degree of privacy from the hostile stares, but instead he paused for a moment, the wicked streak inside him making sure that they had more than enough time to take one more good look at his face. He didn't want there to be any doubt in their minds. He wanted them to know that he was back.

Let them stare and speculate. It would save him the bother of announcing his return.

With a smooth, athletic movement, he settled his powerful body onto the motorbike and caught the eye of the ferryman, acknowledging his disbelieving stare with a slight inclination of his head. He knew exactly what old Jim was thinking—*that the morning ferry had brought trouble to Glenmore.* And news of trouble spread fast on this island. As if to confirm his in-stincts, he caught a few words from the crush of people pre-paring to leave the ferry. *Arrogant, wild, unstable, volatile, handsome as the devil...*

He pushed the helmet down onto his head with his gloved hands. Luckily for him, plenty of women were attracted to arrogant, wild, unstable, volatile men, or his life would have been considerably more boring than it had been.

From behind the privacy of his helmet, he smiled, knowing exactly what would happen next. The rumours would spread like ripples in a pond. Within minutes, news of his arrival would have spread across the island. Ferryman to fisherman, fisherman to shopkeeper, shopkeeper to customer—it would take no time at all for the entire population of the island to be informed of the latest news—that Conner MacNeil had come in on the morning ferry.

The Bad Boy was back on the Island.

CHAPTER ONE

'THE waiting room is packed and you've had five requests for home visits.' Flora handed Logan a prescription to sign, thinking that he looked more tired than ever. 'Given that they were all mobile and none of their complaints sounded life-threatening, Janet's managed to persuade them all to come to the surgery because it just isn't practical for you to go dashing around the island at the moment when you're running this practice on your own. What happens if we have a genuine emergency? You can't be in five places at once. We can't carry on like this, Logan. *You* can't carry on like this. You're going to drop.'

Logan looked at the prescription. 'Gentacin ear drops?'

'Pam King has an infection. She has her ears syringed regularly, but this time the whole of the canal is looking inflamed. There didn't seem any point in adding her to your already buckling list. I've taken off half your patients and if I can sort them out, I will. Otherwise I'll have to push them back through to you.'

'You, Flora Harris, are a miracle.' Logan signed the prescription. 'And persuading you to come back here as my practice nurse was the best thing I ever did. When Kyla and Ethan left, I couldn't imagine how we were going to cope. I lost nurse and doctor in one fell swoop.'

'Well, I've only solved one half of your problem. You still need to find a doctor to replace Ethan. Any progress?'

'I think so.'

'Seriously?' Flora picked the prescription up from his desk. 'You've found someone?'

'Ask me again at lunchtime. I'm expecting someone on the morning ferry.'

'Oh, that's fantastic.' Relieved, Flora relaxed slightly. 'Is he or she good? Well qualified?'

'It's a he.' Logan turned back to his computer. 'And, yes, he's extremely well qualified.'

Flora stared at him expectantly. 'And...?'

'And what?'

'Aren't you going to tell me any more?'

'No.' He tapped a few keys and frowned at the screen. 'How are you finding Glenmore, Flora? I haven't really had a chance to ask you and you've already been here for a month. Everything going all right? Have you settled into Evanna's cottage?'

'Yes, thank you.' *Hadn't they been discussing the new doctor?* Why were they suddenly on the subject of her cottage? Why was he changing the subject? 'Evanna's cottage is beautiful. I love it.' It was true. She'd never imagined she'd live anywhere so pretty. 'You can see the sea from the bed...' she blushed '...but, of course, you already know that, given that the two of you are married. I'm sure you spent plenty of time in her cottage.'

'Actually, we didn't.' Logan glanced at her, amused. 'We usually stayed at mine because there was more room. Are you finding the work very different from the practice in Edinburgh?'

'Not really, but everything takes four times as long because this is Glenmore and people like to chat.' Flora gave a helpless shrug. 'I always seem to be running late.'

'You need to cut them off when they gossip.' Logan turned

his attention back to the computer screen, searching for something. 'That's what the rest of us do.'

'I haven't worked out how to do that without appearing rude. I don't want to offend them. They're all so nice and they mean well.' Flora picked up the prescription and moved towards the door. 'Anyway, I'd better let you carry on. At this rate you'll still be here at midnight. And so will I.'

As she left the room and returned to her own consulting room she suddenly remembered that Logan hadn't given her any more clues as to the identity of the new doctor. On an island where no one kept a secret, Logan appeared to have one. Why? What possible reason could he have for being so cloak and dagger about the whole thing?

Who exactly had he appointed?

Conner parked the motorbike and dragged the helmet from his head. The rain had stopped and the sun fought a battle with the clouds, as if to remind him that the weather on Glenmore Island was as unpredictable as ever.

It was July and still the wind blew.

That same wind had almost landed him in jail at the age of sixteen.

Tucking his helmet under his arm, he strolled into the surgery. *Nice job, Logan*, he thought to himself as he took in his surroundings in one casual glance. Sleek, clean lines and plenty of light. Despite the early hour, the waiting room was already crowded with patients and he saw heads turn and eyes widen as he passed.

Without adjusting his pace, he ignored the reception desk and made for the first consulting room. As he approached the door a patient walked out, clutching a prescription in her hand. She took one look at him and stopped dead, her open mouth reminding him of a baby bird waiting to be fed.

'Conner MacNeil.' Her voice trailed off in a strangled

squeak and he lifted an eyebrow, a sardonic expression in his eyes as he observed her mounting discomfort.

If he'd been in any doubt as to the islanders' reaction to his return, that doubt had now gone.

'Mrs Graham.' He was cool and polite, his neutral tone a direct contrast to her shock and consternation. He moved past her, knowing that he should cut short the encounter, but he couldn't quite help himself and he turned, the devil dancing in his eyes. 'I hope your beautiful garden is thriving. If I remember correctly, it's always at its best in July.'

Her soft gasp of outrage made it obvious that her memories of their last meeting were as clear as his and a smile played around his hard mouth as he walked into the consulting room without bothering to knock.

Mrs Graham's garden.

He still remembered the girl...

He pushed the door shut with the flat of his hand and the man at the desk looked up.

'Conner.' Logan rose to his feet, welcome in his eyes as he stretched out his hand. 'It's been too long.'

'Not long enough for some,' Conner murmured, thinking of Mrs Graham who, he was sure, at that precise moment was still glaring angrily at the closed door. 'Prepare yourself for a riot. The locals will be arming themselves any minute now.' He shook the hand of the man who had been part of his boyhood.

'Kate Graham recognised you, then? I seem to recall that you were stark naked the last time she saw you.'

The devil was back in Conner's eyes. 'Mrs Graham had extremely tall delphiniums in her border,' he recalled. 'She only saw my face.'

Logan laughed out loud. 'You have no idea how pleased I am to see you. You're looking good, Conner.'

'I wish I could return the compliment.' Conner's dark brows drew together in a frown as he studied his cousin, taking in the faint shadows and the lines of strain. 'You've looked better.

Island life obviously doesn't suit you. You need to leave this backwater and find yourself a proper job.' But his tone was light because he knew that the medical care that his cousin delivered on this remote Scottish island was of exceptional quality.

'There's nothing wrong with island life, just the lack of medical staff. To run this place effectively we need two doctors and two nurses.' Logan rubbed his fingers over his forehead. 'It's been tough since Kyla and Ethan left. I lost a doctor and a nurse in one blow.'

Conner thought about his cousin. 'I never thought Kyla would leave this place.'

'She married an Englishman with itchy feet.'

'There's treatment for that.'

'Yeah.' Logan grinned. 'Anyway, it's only temporary and I've replaced Kyla. Now you're here, so we're back on track.'

'If I were you, I'd postpone the celebrations until the whole island gets wind of your little plan. The jungle drums will start beating soon.'

'They're already beating.' Logan picked up his coffee-mug and then realised that it was empty and put it down again. 'My phone has been ringing and you've only been on the island for twenty minutes. You certainly know how to make a lasting impression, Conner MacNeil. What exactly did you do on that ferry?'

'Travelled on it. Apparently that was more than enough.' Conner stretched his legs out in front of him and put his helmet down on the floor. 'There's going to be a rebellion. If looks could kill, I'd be in your mortuary right now, not your consulting room. The natives will probably return to their roots and take up arms to defend themselves from the unwelcome invader. They're preparing themselves for rape and pillage.'

'Ignore them. You know what the islanders are like.' Logan reached for a pack of papers. 'They don't like change. Can you read this lot quickly and sign? Just a formality.'

'And you know how much I love formality,' Connor drawled

softly, but he leaned forward to take the papers, grimacing when he saw the thickness of the documentation. 'Life's too short to wade through that much bureaucracy. What does it say? *Conner MacNeil must not steal, destroy property or otherwise harass the citizens of Glenmore*?'

'All that and the fact that all single women under the age of thirty are now considered to be in danger.' Logan's eyes gleamed as he handed his cousin a pen. 'The men of the island are locking up their wives and daughters as we speak and Mrs Graham is probably shovelling fertiliser on her delphiniums to increase their height and preserve her modesty and yours. Sign the back page.'

'Single women under the age of thirty? Why thirty? That doesn't give me nearly enough scope. I've always preferred experience to innocence.' Conner flipped straight to the back of the sheaf of papers and signed with a casual flourish.

Logan lifted an eyebrow. 'Aren't you going to bother to read what you just signed?'

'I'm presuming it's a load of rules and regulations.'

'And knowing that, you're prepared to sign? I thought you hated rules and regulations.'

'I do, but I trust you and I admire what you've built here on Glenmore.' Conner handed the papers back to Logan, a faint smile on his mouth. 'I promise to do my best for your patients. I'm *not* promising that I won't bend the rules a little if it proves to be necessary.'

Logan reached for an envelope. 'I bend them all the time. It's the only way to get things done. It's good to have you here, Conner.'

'I don't think everyone is going to agree with you. Judging from the shock on the faces I've seen so far, you didn't warn them in advance.'

'Do I look stupid?' Logan slipped the papers into the envelope and dropped it into the tray on his desk. 'I was waiting until you showed up.'

'Did you think I wouldn't?'

'Reliability isn't your middle name. I wasn't sure you'd actually do this when the time came.'

Connor gave a humourless laugh. 'Then that makes two of us.'

'But you did, so now I can break the happy news to the inhabitants of Glenmore. How have you been? Tell me, honestly.' Logan hesitated. 'It must have been hard…'

'Coming back? Why would you say that?' Conner was surprised to find that his voice sounded so harsh. 'You know how much I love this place.'

Ignoring the sarcasm, Logan watched him steadily. 'Actually, I was talking about leaving the army.'

The army?

Conner realised that since he'd stepped off the ferry, he'd given no thought to the life he'd just left. All he could think about was Glenmore and how it felt to be back. The bad memories poured into him like some dark, insidious disease, gradually taking possession of his mind. 'Leaving the army isn't my problem at the moment.' he growled. 'And, anyway, I don't believe in living in the past when there's a perfectly good future to be getting on with.'

'Are you going to sell the house?'

'You get straight to the point, don't you?' Conner rose to his feet and paced across the room, keeping his back to his cousin as he rode the pain. 'Yes.' He turned, his eyes fierce. 'Why would I keep it?'

'So that you have a place on Glenmore?'

'If I'd wanted that,' Conner said softly, 'why would I be renting your barn?'

'Good point.' Logan gave him a sympathetic look. 'This must be hard for you, I know.'

'Nowhere near as hard as it's going to be for the locals.' Conner studied a picture on the wall. 'They're going to think that you've lost your mind, appointing me as the locum.'

'They'd be less shocked if you told them the truth about what you've been doing since you stormed off Glenmore all those years ago.'

'Island gossip has never interested me.'

'You sound like Flora. Her clinics are taking twice as long as they should because she doesn't like to interrupt people when they're chatting.'

'Flora?'

'My practice nurse. She replaced Kyla.'

'Flora Harris?' Conner turned, the pain inside him under control. 'Daughter of Ian Harris, our island solicitor? Niece of our esteemed headmistresses?'

Cloudy dark hair, soft brown eyes, an impossibly shy and awkward teenager, and as innocent as the dawn...

Logan's eyes narrowed. 'You didn't ever...'

'Fortunately for her, there were enough wild teenage girls on the island who were more than happy to experiment, without me having to corrupt the saintly Flora. Anyway, she didn't take her nose out of a book for long enough to discover the existence of sex.'

'She isn't saintly. Just shy.'

'Maybe. But definitely not the sort of girl who would skip classes in favour of a practical session on human reproduction.' Conner rolled his shoulders to ease the tension. 'I'm not surprised she's a nurse. It would have been that or a librarian. Does she know I'm the new doctor?'

'Not yet.'

'She won't approve.'

'Even if she doesn't, she would never say so. Flora is sweet, kind and incredibly civilised.'

'Whereas I'm sharp, unkind and incredibly uncivilised. I'm willing to bet that the first thing she does, when she finds out about me, is remind you that I blew up the science lab.'

'I'd forgotten about that.' Momentarily distracted, Logan narrowed his eyes. 'What did you use—potassium?'

'Too dangerous. They didn't keep it at school.' Restless, Conner paced across the room again and scanned the row of textbooks on the shelf. 'But they did keep sodium. That was good enough.'

'It should have been in a locked cupboard.'

'It was.'

Logan laughed. 'I'm amazed you weren't expelled.'

'Me, too. Very frustrating, given how hard I applied myself to the task.' Conner suppressed a yawn. 'So I'm going to be working with Flora. The excitement of this place increases by the minute.'

'She's a brilliant nurse. She was working in Edinburgh until last month but we persuaded her to come back. And now you've joined us. I've been thinking—we should tell the islanders what you've been doing with your life.'

'It's none of their business.'

Logan sighed. 'I don't see why you're so reluctant to let people know that you're a good guy.'

'Who says I'm a good guy? If you wanted a good guy for the job then you've appointed the wrong man.' Conner turned, a ghost of a smile on his face. 'You'll have a hard job convincing Flora, Mrs Graham and any of that lot on the ferry that there's a single decent bone in my body.'

'Give them time. How soon can you start?'

'That depends on how soon you want to clear out your surgery.' Conner unzipped his jacket. 'I can guarantee that they won't be queuing up to see me. I'm assuming that, by appointing me, you want to encourage your patients to deal with their ailments at home. We both know they won't be coming to the surgery once they know who the doctor is. Which means I get to lounge around all day with my feet up while you pay my salary.'

'That's rubbish. You know as well as I do that the women will be forming a disorderly queue all the way to the harbour.'

Logan's expression was serious. 'Tell them the truth about yourself, Con. It will help them understand you.'

'I don't need them to understand me. That's always been the difference between us. You *are* a nice guy. I'm not. You care about them. I don't.'

'So why are you here?'

'Not out of love for the islanders, that's for sure. And I'm here because…' Conner shrugged '…you rang me. I came. Let's leave it at that.' He didn't want to think about the rest of it. Not yet. He frowned, his attention caught by one of the photographs on the wall. 'Isn't that little Evanna Duncan? Are you two together?'

'She's Evanna MacNeil now,' Logan's tone was a shade cooler as he corrected him. 'I married her a year ago and if you so much as glance in her direction you might just discover that I'm not such a nice guy after all.'

'Seducing married women has never been on my list of vices.' Conner turned and looked at his cousin. 'She always adored you. Children?'

'Evanna is due in five weeks.' Logan hesitated. 'And I have a daughter from a previous marriage. Kirsty. She's two.'

'So, you're a regular family man.' Conner saw the shadows in Logan's eyes but he knew better than to ask questions. He had plenty of shadows of his own, *dark corners that he kept private.*

Logan's gaze didn't waver. 'What about you? Wife? Children?'

'I'll assume that wasn't a serious question.'

'I was just hoping you had a reason not to wreak havoc across the female population of Glenmore over the summer. Just don't touch the patients, it's strictly frowned on and definitely against the rules.' Logan rose to his feet. 'Use the consulting room across the corridor. Do you want to shave or change before you start?'

'And ruin the opportunity to shock everyone? I don't think so. I'll stay as I am.'

'I've just broken the news of your arrival to Janet, our receptionist. She's already lined up some patients. Is there anything you need to know before you start?'

'Yes.' Conner paused, his hand on the door. 'If I'm not allowed to seduce the patients, how am I supposed to relieve the boredom of being trapped on Glenmore?'

'I don't suppose you'd consider a round of golf?'

'No.'

'I didn't think you would. Well, I'm confident you'll find something or someone to distract you.' Logan gave a resigned laugh. 'Just steer clear of Mrs Graham's garden, that's all I ask.'

She needed to talk to Logan quickly.

Flora nipped across the corridor and tapped lightly on the door. Without waiting for an answer, she walked into his consulting room and immediately collided with a tall, dark-haired man whose body seemed to be made of nothing but rock-hard muscle. She stumbled slightly but his hands came out and steadied her, his strong fingers digging into her arms as he held her.

'I'm *terribly* sorry,' she apologised breathlessly, catching her glasses before they could slide down her nose, 'I had no idea Logan had a patient with him.'

'Hello, Flora.' His lazy, masculine drawl was alarmingly familiar and her eyes flew wide as she tilted her head back to take a proper look at him.

'Oh!' Her heart started to beat in double time and she felt decidedly faint. Her knees weakened and from a distance she heard Logan's voice.

'Flora, you remember my cousin Conner?'

Remember? *Remember?* Well, of course she remembered! She might be short-sighted, but she was still a woman! And it didn't matter how many rules or hearts he'd broken, there wasn't a woman alive who would forget Conner MacNeil once she'd met him.

Especially not her.

And he would have known how she'd felt because arrogance and Conner had gone hand in hand. Even as a young boy he'd known exactly what effect he had on the girls and had used it to his advantage.

But it wasn't a boy who was standing in front of her now. It was a man. And his effect on the opposite sex had grown proportionately.

Determined not to boost his ego by revealing her thoughts, Flora screwed up her face and adopted what she hoped was a puzzled expression. 'Conner…Conner… The name *is* familiar—were you below me at school? Or were you above me?'

His blue eyes glinted with wicked humour. 'I don't recall ever being above or below you, Flora,' he murmured softly, 'but that may be my defective memory.'

She felt the heat flare in her cheeks and remembered, too late, that anyone trying to play word games with Conner was always going to lose. His brain and his tongue worked in perfect unison whereas hers had always been slightly disconnected. Without fail she thought of the perfect thing to say about two days after the opportunity to say it had passed.

'Well, you do look vaguely familiar,' she said quickly, stepping back and concentrating her attention on Logan to cover up how unsettled she felt. A moment ago she'd been happily existing in the present, enjoying her life. The next she'd been transported back to her childhood and it was a lonely, uncomfortable place. If this was time travel, then she wanted none of it.

She'd had such a desperate, agonising crush on Conner. *A crush that had been intensified by the fact that her father had forbidden her to mix with him.* 'Sorry to disturb your reunion, but Amy Price just rang me. Heather has chickenpox.'

'And?' Logan frowned. 'Tell her to buy some paracetamol and chlorpheniramine from the pharmacy.'

'I'm not worried about Heather. I'm worried about your wife. Evanna saw the child in clinic yesterday.'

'And the child would have been infectious.' Understanding dawned and Logan cursed softly. 'Has Evanna had chickenpox?'

'I don't think so. That's why I thought you ought to know straight away. I remember talking about it with her a few months ago. She was telling me that her mother sent her off to play with everyone who had chickenpox, but she never caught it.'

'Chickenpox is a disease that you don't want to catch in the third trimester of pregnancy.'

'That's what I thought.'

Somehow she was managing to have a normal conversation with Logan, but her head and senses were filled with Conner. In some ways he'd changed, she mused, and yet in others he hadn't. The muscular physique was the reward of manhood but other things—*the air of supreme indifference and the ice-blue eyes*—had been part of the boy.

What was he doing here, anyway? Like everyone else, she'd assumed he'd never show his face on the island again.

Logan walked to his desk. 'I'll call Evanna now.'

'I've already done it. She's about to start her clinic, but she'll come and talk to you first. I thought you might want to delay your first patient or pass him across to the new doctor when he arrives.'

'Relax. She's probably immune.' Conner leaned his broad shoulders against the doorframe, watching them both with an expression that could have been amusement or boredom. 'Do a blood test and check her antibody status.'

She was wrong, Flora realised with a flash of disquiet. *There was nothing of the boy left.* There were more changes than she'd thought, and some were so subtle that they weren't immediately obvious. Those ice-blue eyes were sharper and more cynical, and his arrogance had clearly developed along with his muscles. *What did he know about antibody status?* Or was he one of those people who watched all the medical soaps on television and then assumed they were qualified to diagnose?

To make matters worse, Logan was nodding, encouraging him. 'Yes—yes, I'll do that, but if she's not immune...'

'Then you just give her zoster immunoglobulin. What's the matter with you?' Conner's brows drew into a frown as he looked at his cousin. 'This is why I'm careful not to fall in love. It fries your brain cells and obliterates your judgement.'

'There's nothing wrong with Logan's judgement.' Fiercely loyal, Flora immediately flew to Logan's defence and then wished she hadn't because Conner switched his gaze from Logan to her and his attention was unsettling, to say the least.

Apparently unaware of the change in the atmosphere, Logan rubbed his hand over the back of his neck. 'When you love someone, Conner,' he said, 'you lose perspective.'

Conner's eyes held Flora's. 'I wouldn't know. That's one mistake I've never made.'

She swallowed, every bit as uncomfortable as he'd clearly intended her to be. Was he trying to shock her? He'd had women, she knew that. Probably many. Was she surprised that he'd never found love? *That he considered love a mistake?*

'True love is a gift, given to few,' she murmured, and Conner's mouth tilted and his blue eyes glinted with sardonic humour.

'True love is a curse, bestowed on the unlucky. Love brings weakness and vulnerability. How can that be a gift?'

Flustered, she cleared her throat and looked away. *What was he doing here?* Why had he returned to Glenmore with no warning, looking like the bad guy out of a Hollywood movie? His hair was dark and cropped short and his jaw was dark with stubble. He was *indecently* handsome and the only thing that marred the otherwise faultless symmetry of his features was the slight bump in his nose, an imperfection which she assumed to be the legacy of a fight. He looked tough and dangerous and the impression of virile manhood was further intensified by the width and power of his shoulders under the black leather jacket.

He wasn't attractive, Flora told herself desperately. How could he possibly be attractive? He looked…rough. Rough and a little menacing. She thought of the conventional, bespectacled lawyer she'd dated for a while in Edinburgh. He'd always let her through doors first and had been completely charming. His hair had always been neat and tidy and she'd never, ever seen him anything other than clean-shaven. He'd almost always worn a suit when they'd dated and his legs hadn't filled his trousers the way that Conner's did. And then there had been his smile. His cheeks had dimpled slightly and his eyes had been kind. *Nothing like Conner's eyes.* Conner's eyes were fierce and hard, as if he was just waiting for someone to pick a fight so that he could work off some pent-up energy.

Her heart thudded hard against her chest. Conner MacNeil wasn't charming or kind. He was—He was…unsuitable. Dangerous. A woman had to be mad to look twice at a man like him.

Why, she wondered helplessly, *was the unsuitable and the dangerous always so much more appealing than the suitable?*

'We need to get on.' With a huge effort of will, she broke the connection and turned her attention back to Logan. 'We've a busy surgery this morning. What happened to the new doctor? Did he show up? You didn't tell me who he is or when he or she can start.'

'You heard the woman.' Logan turned to Conner. 'Go and do your job.'

Conner shrugged and a slight smile touched his mouth. 'Prepare for chaos.'

It took Flora a moment to understand the implications of their conversation. 'You can't— Conner?' Her voice cracked.

'But Conner isn't—' She broke off and Conner lifted an eyebrow.

'Don't stop there,' he prompted softly. 'I'm keen to hear all the things I'm not.'

Not suitable. Not safe. Not conventional. Not responsible... She could have drawn up a never-ending list of things he was not. 'I—You're not a doctor. You *can't* be a doctor.'

He smiled. 'Why? Because I didn't hand in my homework on time?'

'You didn't hand in your homework at all. You were hardly ever at school!'

'I'm flattered that you noticed.' His soft observation was a humiliating reminder that she'd always been aware of him and he'd never even noticed her.

She was probably the only girl on Glenmore who hadn't been kissed by Conner MacNeil.

She turned away, horrified that after all this time she still cared that she'd been invisible to him. 'You're forgetting that my aunt was the headmistress.'

'I've forgotten nothing.' There was something in his tone that made her glance at him and speculate. There was resentment there and—*anger*?

He'd always seemed angry, she remembered. *Angry, moody and wild.*

Was that why he was back? Was he seeking revenge on the people who had disapproved and eventually despaired of him?

'Ann runs a wonderful school.' She felt compelled to defend her family. 'The children all adore her and they get a fantastic education.'

'There's more to education than sitting in rows in a class-room with a book in front of you.' Conner leaned nonchalantly against the table, his glance speculative. 'Still the same Flora. Conventional. Playing everything by the rules. I presume that all your affairs are still with books?'

His comment stung. He made her feel so—so—*boring*. Plain, boring Flora. And that was what they'd called her at school, of course. *Boring Flora.* Hurt, she clawed back. 'Rules are there for a reason and if you're really a doctor then I hope you've read a few books yourself along the way, otherwise I pity your patients.' She stopped, shocked at herself and aware that Logan was gaping at her in amazement.

'Flora! I've never heard you speak to anyone like that before. Usually I have to drag a response from you. What is the matter with you?'

'I don't know. I— Nothing.' Flora's cheeks were scarlet and she blinked several times and adjusted her glasses. She didn't know what was the matter. She didn't know what had come over her. *She didn't know why she felt so hot and bothered.* 'Sorry. I apologise.'

She felt miserably uncomfortable and mortified that she'd embarrassed Logan. The only person who didn't seem remotely embarrassed was Conner himself. He simply laughed.

'Don't apologise. I much prefer to be around people who say what they think. I'm sure most of the inhabitants of Glenmore will share your sentiments and express them far more vociferously.' He turned to Logan. 'I did warn you that this wouldn't work. It isn't too late to change your mind.'

'Of course I'm not going to change my mind.' Logan sounded exasperated. 'Flora, Conner's credentials are—'

'Irrelevant,' Conner interrupted smoothly, and Flora bit her lip.

She knew she ought to say something nice and welcoming, but her brain just didn't seem to be working with its normal efficiency. Seeing Conner again without warning was shocking, confusing and—*thrilling*?

Horrified, she quickly dismissed that last emotion and pressed her fingers to her chest, wishing that her heart would slow down. It was not, definitely not, thrilling that he was back on the island. If she'd been asked to choose the least suitable man to be a doctor on Glenmore, it would have been Conner MacNeil.

Over the years, she'd thought of him often.

Too often.

She'd wondered where he was and what he was doing. She'd imagined him languishing in some jail, maybe in a foreign country; she'd imagined him sitting by a pool in a tax haven, having made piles of money by some unspeakably dubious means.

Never, in her most extravagant fantasies, had she imagined him training as a doctor and never, in those same dreams, had she imagined him returning to Glenmore.

One thing she knew for sure; the calm, tranquil routine of Glenmore Island was about to be overturned.

She didn't know what sort of doctor Conner was going to prove to be, but she knew it wasn't the sort that the islanders were used to seeing.

CHAPTER TWO

CONNER buzzed for his first patient and braced himself for the reaction.

He wasn't disappointed.

The first man who walked through his door took one look at him, gave a horrified gasp and immediately backed out, muttering that he'd 'wait for the other doctor'.

Conner watched him leave, his handsome face expressionless. Clearly people had long memories and he understood all about that. *He hadn't forgotten a single minute of his time on Glenmore.*

With a dismissive shrug, he buzzed for the next patient and the moment Susan Ellis walked through the door, he prepared himself for a repeat performance. If he had any supporters among the islanders—*and he was beginning to doubt that he had*—this lady wouldn't be among them. She ran the shop at the harbour and she had reason to know him better than most.

'Good morning, Mrs Ellis.' He kept his tone suitably neutral but her face reflected her shock at seeing him.

'Conner MacNeil! So the rumours are true, then.' She glanced behind her, obviously wondering if she'd wandered into the wrong building, and Conner lifted an eyebrow.

'Is there something I can help you with, Mrs Ellis?' *Perhaps this wasn't going to work after all.*

'I don't know. I'll have to think about it.'

It was on the tip of his tongue to tell her to think quickly because there was a queue of patients waiting but then he realised that the queue was probably dwindling by the second so a slightly longer consultation wasn't likely to matter.

'If you'd rather see Logan, go ahead. My feelings will remain intact.'

'I'm not thinking about your feelings,' she said tartly. 'I'm thinking about my health. I assume Logan knows you're here?'

'You think I broke a window and climbed in? Looking for drugs, maybe?'

She gave him a reproving look. 'Don't give me sarcasm, Conner MacNeil. I'm not afraid to admit that you wouldn't leap to mind as someone to turn to in times of trouble.'

Clearly recalling the details of their last encounter, Conner relented slightly. 'I don't blame you for that.'

She studied him from the safety of the doorway, her mouth compressed into a firm line of disapproval. 'So you've mended your ways. Are you really a doctor?'

'Apparently.'

'There's plenty on this island who will be surprised to hear that.'

'I'm sure that's true.' Conner kept his tone level. 'Are you going or staying? Because if you're staying, you may as well sit down. Or we can carry on this consultation standing, up if that's what you would prefer.'

'Not very friendly, are you?'

'I presumed you were looking for a doctor, not a date.'

Susan Ellis gave a reluctant laugh. 'You always were a sharp one, I'll give you that.' After a moment's hesitation she closed the door and sat down gingerly on the edge of the seat, as if she hadn't quite decided whether she was going to stay or not. 'I'm not sure if I can talk about this with you.'

Conner sighed. *It was going to be a long day.* 'As I said, if you'd rather see Logan, I quite understand.'

She fiddled with the strap of her handbag and then put it on the floor in a decisive movement. 'No,' she said firmly. 'I've never been one to live in the past. Times change. People change. If you're a doctor then— I don't suppose you'll be able to help me anyway.'

'Try me.'

'It's hard to put a finger on when it all started, but it's been a while.' She glanced at Conner and he sat in silence, just listening. 'Probably been almost a year. I'm tired, you see. All the time. And I know doctors hate hearing that. You're going to say it's just my age, but—'

'I haven't said anything yet, Mrs Ellis. You speak your lines and then I'll speak mine.' He could have been wrong but he thought he saw her shoulders relax slightly.

'Fair enough. Well, I feel washed out and exhausted a lot of the time. It doesn't matter how well I sleep or how much rest I take, I'm still tired.' She hesitated and then sighed. 'And a little depressed, if I'm honest. But that's probably because I just feel so…slow. If this is getting old, I want none of it.'

'Have you gained weight?'

She stiffened. 'Are you going to lecture me on my eating?'

'Are you going to answer the question?'

Susan shifted self consciously, automatically pulling in her stomach and straightening her shoulders. 'Yes, I've gained weight, but I suppose that's my age as well. You just can't eat so much when you get older and it's hard to change old habits. Aren't you going to make notes? Logan always keeps meticulous notes.'

'I prefer to listen. I'll do the writing part later.' Conner stood up and walked towards her, his eyes concentrating on her face. 'Your skin is dry. Is that usual for you?'

'Didn't used to be but it's usual now. My hair's the same.' She tilted her face so that he could take a closer look. 'Observant, aren't you?'

'Sometimes.' Having looked at her skin, Conner took her hands in his and examined them carefully. Then he looked at her eyelids. 'You have slight oedema. Can I take a look at your feet?'

'My feet?'

'That's right.' He squatted down and helped her slip her shoes off.

'I never thought I'd have Conner MacNeil at my feet.'

'Savour the moment, Mrs Ellis. Do they bother you?'

'They're aching terribly and I wouldn't be surprised if they're a bit swollen…' She wiggled her toes. 'I assumed it was the heat.'

Conner examined her feet and ankles. 'From what I've seen, Glenmore is in the middle of a typical summer. Wind and rain. I'm not expecting any cases of heatstroke today.' He was sure that her feet were swollen for a very different reason.

'We had sunshine last week. You know Glenmore—the weather is always unpredictable. A bit like you.' She looked at him, her gaze slightly puzzled. 'You're very gentle. I hadn't expected that of you.'

'I prefer not to leave marks on my victims.' A faint smile on his face, Conner rose to his feet. 'The swelling isn't caused by heat, Mrs Ellis. I can tell you that much.' He washed his hands and picked up the IV tray that Flora had left on the trolley. 'I'm going to take some blood.'

'Is that really necessary?'

'No. I just want to cause you pain.'

His patient laughed out loud. 'Revenge, Conner?'

'Maybe. You called the police that night.'

'Yes, I did.' Susan stuck out her arm. 'You were out of control. Only eight years old and helping yourself to what you wanted from my shop.'

He ran his fingers gently over her skin, searching for a vein. 'I needed some stuff and I didn't have the money to pay.'

'And how often did I hear that from the children? Plenty of them did it.' Her laughter faded and she shook her head as she watched him. 'But I remember you. You were different. So bold. A real rebel. Even when John, our island policeman, gave you a talking to, you didn't cry. It was as if you were used to being shouted at. As if you'd hardened yourself.'

Conner didn't falter. 'You have good veins. This shouldn't be hard.'

'You're not going to excuse yourself, are you?'

'Why would I do that?'

'Because we found out later that there were things happening in your house.' She spoke softly. 'Plenty to explain why you were the way you were.'

Suddenly the room felt bitterly cold. Conner slipped a tourniquet over her wrist. 'Everyone's family is complicated. Mine was no different.'

'No?' Susan looked at him for a moment and then sighed. 'I remember how you looked on that day. You just stood there, all defiant, your chin up and those blue eyes of yours flashing daggers. Oh, you were angry with me.'

'As you said, you'd called the police.'

'But it didn't have any effect. You were never afraid of anyone or anything, were you, Conner MacNeil?'

Oh, yes, he'd been afraid. *'Don't do it. Don't touch her—I'll kill you if you touch her.'*

With ruthless determination Conner pushed the memory back into the darkness where it belonged. 'On the contrary, I was afraid of my cousin Kyla.' Keeping his tone neutral, he tightened the tourniquet and studied the woman's veins. 'She had a deadly punch and a scream that would puncture your eardrums.'

'Ah, Kyla. We all miss her. It's not good when islanders leave. It's not good for Glenmore.'

Swift and sure, Conner slipped the needle into the vein. 'Depends on the islander, Mrs Ellis. There are some people that Glenmore is pleased to see the back of.' He released the tourniquet and watched as the blood flowed. 'I'm checking your thyroid function, by the way.'

'Oh. Why?'

'Because I think hypothyroidism is a possible explanation for your symptoms.' Having collected the blood he needed, he withdrew the needle and covered the area with a pad. 'Press on that for a moment, would you? If you leave here with bruises, that will be another black mark against me.'

She looked down at her arm. 'That's it? You've finished? You're good at that. I barely felt it.' The expression in her eyes cooled. 'I suppose you have a lot of experience with needles.'

Conner picked up a pen and labelled the bottles. 'I'm the first to admit that my list of vices is deplorably long, Mrs Ellis, but I've never done drugs.'

Her shoulders relaxed. 'I'm sorry,' she said softly. 'That was uncalled for. If I've offended you…'

'You haven't offended me.' He dropped the blood samples into a bag, wondering what had possessed him to take the job on Glenmore. He could have come in on the ferry, sorted out his business and left again.

'Hypothyroidism, you say?'

'There are numerous alternative explanations, of course, but this is a good place to start.'

'I don't know whether to be relieved or alarmed. I was expecting you to tell me it was nothing. Should I be worried?'

'Worrying doesn't achieve anything. If we find a problem, we'll look for a solution.' He completed the necessary form and then washed his hands again. 'I'm going to wait for those results before we look at anything else because I have a strong feeling that we've found the culprit.'

'You're confident.'

'Would you prefer me to fumble and dither?'

She laughed. 'You always were a bright boy, Conner MacNeil. Too bright, some would say. Bright and a rebel. A dangerous combination.'

Conner sat back down in his chair. 'Call the surgery in three days for the result and then make another appointment to see me. We can talk about what to do next.'

'All right, I'll do that. Thank you.' Susan picked up her bag, rose to her feet and walked to the door. Then she turned. 'I always regretted it, you know.'

Conner looked up. 'Regretted what?'

'Calling the police.' Her voice was soft. 'At the time I thought you needed a fright. I thought a bit of discipline might sort you out. But I was wrong. You were wild. Out of control. But what you needed was a bit of love. People to believe in you. I see that now. What with everything that was happening at home—your mum and dad. Of course, none of us knew the details at the time, but—'

'You did the right thing calling the police, Mrs Ellis,' Conner said in a cool tone. 'In your position I would have called them, too.'

'At the time I was angry that they didn't charge you.'

'I'm sure you were.'

It was her turn to smile. 'Now I'm pleased they didn't. Can I ask you something?'

'You can ask. I don't promise to answer.'

'There was a spate of minor shoplifting at that time but everyone else was taking sweets and crisps. You took the oddest assortment of things. What did you want it all for?'

Conner leaned back and smiled. 'I was making a bomb.'

'He blew up the science lab!' Flora stood in front of Logan, trying to make him to see reason.

'Funny.' Logan scanned the lab result in front of him. 'Conner said that you'd bring that up.'

'Of course I'm bringing it up. It says everything about the type of person he is.'

'Was.' Logan lifted his eyes to hers. 'It tells you who he was. Not who he is.'

'You really think he's changed?'

'Are you the same person you were at fifteen?'

Agonisingly shy, barely able to string a sentence together in public. Flora flushed. 'No,' she said huskily. 'Of course not.'

Logan shrugged. 'Perhaps he's changed, too.'

'And what if he hasn't? What sort of doctor is he going to make?'

'An extremely clever one. Most people wouldn't have had such a good understanding of the reactivity series to cause that explosion. Anyway, I thought you were relieved that I'd found another doctor.'

'I was, but I never thought for a moment it would be— I mean, *Conner*?' Flora's expression was troubled. 'He's right, you know. The locals won't be happy. What if they make life difficult for him?'

'They always did. He'll cope. Conner is as tough as they come.'

'I can't believe he's a doctor. How did you find out? I mean, he vanished without trace.'

'I stayed in touch with him.' Logan lifted his gaze to hers. 'He's my cousin, Flora. Family. I knew he was a doctor. When I knew I needed help, he seemed the obvious choice.'

'Are you sure? He used to be very unstable. Unreliable. Rebellious. Disruptive.' *Attractive, compelling, addictive.*

'You're describing the teenager.'

'He created havoc.' she looked at him, wondering why she had to remind him of something that he must know himself. 'He was suspended from school *three times*. If there'd been an alternative place for him to go, I'm sure he would have been expelled. Not only did he blow up the science lab, he set off a firework in the library, he burned down the MacDonalds' barn—the list of things he did is endless. He was wild, Logan. Totally out of control.' *And impossibly, hopelessly attractive.* There hadn't been a woman on Glenmore who hadn't dreamed of taming him. Herself included.

She'd wanted to help.

She'd wanted...

She pushed the thought away quickly. She'd been a dreamy teenager but she was an adult now, a grown woman and far too sensible to see Conner as anything other than a liability.

'His parents were going through a particularly acrimonious divorce at the time. There were lots of rumours about that household. My aunt—his mother—left when he was eleven. That's tough on any child.' Logan turned his attention back to the pile in his in-tray. 'Enough to shake the roots of any family. It's not surprising he was disruptive.'

'He isn't interested in authority.'

Logan threw the pen down on his desk. 'Perhaps he thinks that those in authority let him down.'

Flora bit her lip. 'Perhaps they did. But if that's the case then it makes even less sense that he's back. He couldn't wait to get away from Glenmore the first time around and he stayed away for *twelve years*.'

'Is it that long?' Logan studied her face thoughtfully. 'I haven't been counting, but obviously you have.'

'It was a wild guess,' Flora muttered quickly, 'but either way, it's been a long time. And the question is, why has he picked this particular moment to come back?'

'Why does it matter? If he turns out to be a lousy doctor, I'm the one who will pay the price. Or is there more to this than your concern for the reputation of Glenmore Medical Centre? Is this personal, Flora?' Logan's voice was gentle. 'Is there something going on that I should know about?'

'Don't be ridiculous.' Flora rose to her feet swiftly, her heart pounding. 'And I think it's obvious to everyone that I'm not his type. I've never been attracted to unsuitable men.' A painful lump sat in the pit of her stomach. *He'd never looked at her. Not once.*

'Then you're probably the only woman on the island who wasn't,' Logan said mildly, 'if I recall correctly, Conner had quite a following, and the more reprehensible his behaviour, the bigger the following.'

'I suppose some of the girls found him attractive because he was forbidden territory.' Flora wished her heart would slow down. 'I still can't believe he's a doctor.'

'I know you can't. You didn't exactly hide your astonishment,' Logan said dryly and Flora felt a twinge of guilt.

'I didn't mean to be rude but weren't *you* surprised when you found out?'

'No.' Logan rolled his shoulders to ease the stiffness of sitting. 'Conner always was ferociously clever.'

'He hated school. He was barely ever there.'

'And he still managed straight As in every subject. As I said—we all let him down. He was too clever to be trapped behind a desk and forced to learn in a prescribed pattern. People were too conventional to notice the brain behind the behavioural problems.'

Flora gave a puzzled frown. She'd never thought of it that way before. 'Well, he obviously learned to study at some point. Where did he train, anyway?'

'In the army.'

'In the—' Stunned, Flora swallowed. 'He was in the *army*?'

'Army medic.' Logan flipped through a pile of papers on his desk and removed a file. 'Read.' He handed it to her. 'It's impressive stuff. Perhaps it will set your mind at rest about his ability and dedication.'

'But the army requires discipline. All the things Conner doesn't—'

'*Read*,' Logan said firmly. 'The patients might doubt him to begin with, but I don't want the practice staff making the same mistake. The man's qualifications and experience are better than mine. Read, Flora.'

Flora opened the file reluctantly. After a moment, she looked up. 'He's a surgeon?'

'Among other things. I did tell you that the man was clever.'

Her eyes flickered back to the page. 'Afghanistan? That doesn't sound very safe.'

'No.' Logan's voice was dry. 'But it sounds very Conner. I don't suppose anything safe would hold his interest for long.'

'Which brings me back to my original question.' She dropped the file back on his desk. 'What's he doing back on Glenmore? He hates Glenmore and if he still needs adrenaline and excitement in his life, he's going to last five minutes on this island.'

'I don't think it's any of my business.' Logan leaned back in his chair. 'He's back, that's all I need to know.'

'It's going to be like putting a match to a powder keg. And I'm just worried he'll let you down in the middle of the summer tourist season. You and all the islanders.'

Logan's gaze followed her. 'They let him down. This is his chance to even the score or prove himself. Either way, he's family, Flora, and I'm giving him this opportunity. It's up to him what he chooses to do with it.'

Flora bit her lip. Family. On Glenmore family and community was everything. It was what made the island what it was. But Conner had rejected everything that Glenmore stood for. He'd walked away from it.

So why was he back?

CHAPTER THREE

CONNER WATCHED as Flora entered the room. Her eyes were down and she was clutching a bunch of forms that he assumed were for him.

Probably from Logan, he thought, *finding an excuse to engineer peace.*

The fact that she seemed reluctant to look in his direction amused him. As a teenager she'd been impossibly shy. He remembered her sitting on her own in the corner of the playground, her nose stuck in a book. What he didn't remember was her ever stringing more than two words together. But today, in Logan's surgery, she'd been surprisingly articulate.

He gave a cynical smile.

It seemed his presence was enough to encourage even the mute to speak.

'The lamb enters the wolf's den unprotected,' he drawled softly, and watched as the heat built in her cheeks. 'I never saw you as a risk-taker, Flora. Aren't you afraid I might do something evil to you now we're on our own?'

'Don't be ridiculous.' She adjusted her glasses and put the forms on his desk. 'Logan wanted you to have these.'

No, Conner thought to himself. *Logan wanted us to have a moment together because he doesn't want his staff at odds with each other.*

He heard her take a deep breath and then she looked at him.

As if she'd been plucking up courage.

'So…' She cleared her throat. 'How is it going? Any problems so far?'

'No problems at all. The locals are refusing to see me, which means I don't have to spend my time listening to the boring detail of people's minor ailments.' He studied the slight fullness of her lower lip and the smooth curve of her cheeks. *She was pretty*, he realised with a stab of shock. She was also wonderfully, deliciously serious and he couldn't resist having a little fun with her. 'And it's really interesting to make contact with all the girls I…grew up with.'

As he'd anticipated, she flushed. What he hadn't expected was the sudden flash of concern in her eyes. *The kindness.* 'The patients are refusing to see you?' She sounded affronted. 'That's awful.'

'Don't worry about it. I'm allergic to hard work and it gives me more time to spend on the internet.'

'You're just saying that, but you must feel terrible about it.'

'I don't give a damn.'

She gave a faint gasp and blinked several times. 'You don't need to pretend with me. I'm sure you're upset. How could you not be?'

'Flora,' he interrupted her, amused by her misinterpretation of the facts, 'don't endow me with qualities that I don't possess. To feel terrible I'd have to care, and I think we both know that my relationship with the islanders is hardly one of lasting affection.'

'You're very hard on them and perhaps that's justified, but you need to see it from their point of view. Everyone's a bit shocked, that's all. No one was expecting you because Logan didn't say anything to anyone.'

'Given that this is Glenmore, I expect he'll be struck off for respecting confidentiality.'

Her sudden smile caught him by surprise. 'They do gossip, don't they? Everything takes three times as long here because of the conversation. I can't get used to it.' Her smile faded. 'Logan told me about what you've done—your training. That's amazing. I had no idea.'

Conner sat in silence and she spread her hands, visibly uncomfortable with the situation.

'I'm *trying* to apologise. I didn't mean to be rude. It was just that…' She gave an awkward shrug. 'Anyway, I really am sorry.'

'Never apologise, Flora.'

'If I'm wrong, then I apologise,' she said firmly. 'Don't you?'

'I don't know.' Enjoying himself, he smiled. 'I've never been wrong.'

Derailed by the banter, she backed away slightly and then stopped. 'I'm apologising for assuming that you weren't qualified for the job. For thinking that you being here would just cause trouble.'

'It *will* cause trouble,' Conner drawled softly, 'so you weren't wrong.'

'You knew it would cause trouble?'

'Of course.'

His answer brought a puzzled frown to her face. 'If you knew that, why did you come back?'

'I thrive on trouble, Flora. Trouble is the fuel the drives my engine.'

This time, instead of backing away, she looked at him. Properly. Her eyes focused on his, as if she was searching for something. 'You're angry with us, aren't you? Is that why you're here?' She fiddled with her glasses again, as if she wasn't used to having them on her nose. 'To level a score?'

'You think I became a doctor so that I could return to my roots and exterminate the inhabitants of Glenmore, one by one?'

'Of course not. But I know you're angry. I can feel it.'

Then she was more intuitive than he'd thought. Raising his guard, Conner watched her. 'I'm not angry. If people would rather wait a week to see Logan, that's fine by me.'

'But it must hurt your feelings.'

'I don't have feelings, Flora. Providing I still get paid, I don't care whether the patients see me or not. It's Logan's problem.' He could tell she didn't like his answer because she frowned and shook her head slightly.

'I can't believe that you're not at all sensitive about the way people react to you.'

'That's because you're a woman and women think differently to men.' This time his smile was genuine. 'Do I look sensitive?' He watched as her eyes drifted to his shoulders and then lifted to his jaw line.

'No.' Her voice was hoarse. 'You don't.' And then her eyes lifted to his and the atmosphere snapped taut.

Conner felt his body stir.

Well, well, he thought. *How interesting.* Sexual chemistry with a woman who probably didn't know the meaning of the phrase. His gaze lowered to her mouth and he saw that her lips were soft and bare of make-up. He had a sudden impulse to be unforgivably shocking and kiss her.

'Well, if you're sure you're fine…' She was flustered. He could tell she was flustered.

Normally he had no qualms about making a woman flustered but somehow with Flora it seemed unsporting. She might be older but she obviously wasn't any more experienced. With an inner sigh and lingering regret, he backed off. 'I'm fine,' he said gently. 'But thank you for asking.'

He wondered idly if she'd ever had sex.

A boyfriend?

'My consulting room is next door.' Apparently unaware of what had just happened between them, she suddenly became brisk and efficient. 'Evanna is still doing a morning clinic, but if you need a nurse to do a home visit then ask me because she's too pregnant to be dashing around the island. You know your way around, so that shouldn't be a problem. If there's anything you're not sure of, ask.'

'I'll do that.'

If she had a boyfriend, it was someone tame and safe, he decided. Someone who hadn't taught her the meaning of passion.

'Well—I've held you up long enough. Morning surgery can be a long one.' Her gaze slid to his legs, encased in black leather. 'You know, people might feel more comfortable with you if you changed.'

'I am who I am, Flora.'

'I meant your clothes.' She pushed her glasses onto the bridge of her nose. 'You could change your clothes.'

'Why would I want to do that?'

'Because the patients expect a doctor to look like a doctor.'

'Flora.' He failed to keep the amusement out of his voice. 'It wouldn't matter whether I was wearing a set of theatre scrubs or a white coat, the inhabitants of Glenmore would still struggle to believe that Bad Conner is a doctor. Just as *you're* struggling.'

'I'm not. Not any more. But I don't see why you should confirm their prejudices by dressing like a biker.' She flushed. 'Do you always have to antagonise people? Break the rules?'

'Yes. I think I probably do.' Conner watched her. 'Just as you always like to please people and do everything that is expected of you. In our own ways we're the same, you and I. We're both working hard to meet society's expectations of us.'

She looked at him, her dark eyes reproachful. 'There's nothing wrong in being part of a community.'

'True. But neither is there anything wrong with not being part of it,' he said gently. 'Do you really think the way I'm dressed is going to compromise my ability as a doctor?'

'No. Of course not. It's just that you look—' She broke off and he knew he shouldn't follow up on that comment but he couldn't help himself.

'How do I look, Flora? Tell me. I want to know what you think of the way I look.'

She looked hot and flustered. 'I-intimidating,' she stammered, eventually. 'I wouldn't want to bump into you on a dark night.'

'Is that right?' Conner gave a slow smile and gave up trying to subdue his wicked streak. 'In that case, we'll have to make sure that we leave the lights on, angel.'

He was impossible and she was never going to be able to work with him.

Flora tried to concentrate on the dressing and not reveal how shaken she was by her encounter with Conner. He'd played with her, toyed with her carelessly, like a predator having fun with its prey before a kill. And as usual she hadn't been able to think of the right thing to say because she'd been trying to sort out surgery business and he'd been—well, he'd been Conner. Selfish, indifferent and supremely cool. Just the thought of him seeing patients—*or not seeing patients*—in the room next door unsettled her.

She shook her head and studied the skin around the leg ulcer. 'You still have a degree of varicose eczema, Mrs Parker. Are you using the cream Dr MacNeil gave you?'

'The steroid cream? No, I forget.'

Flora studied the skin, checking for infection. 'Is this tender when I press?'

'No more than usual.'

'There's no erythema and your temperature is fine.' Talking to herself, Flora made a judgement. 'We'll leave it for now but do me a favour and try the cream, would you? If it isn't looking better in a week or so, I'm going to ask one of the doctors to look at it.'

'As long as it's Logan.' Mrs Parker's mouth clamped in a thin line of disapproval. 'I'm not afraid to say that I almost fainted dead away when I saw Conner MacNeil stroll into the surgery this morning. Bold as brass. Not even trying to hide his face.'

'Why would he hide his face, Mrs Parker?' Flora swiftly finished the dressing and applied a compression bandage. 'He's a doctor and he's come to—' *create havoc?* '—help Logan.'

'Help? Help? This is the boy who was so much of a handful that his mother left home! Can you imagine how badly the boy must have behaved for his own mother to give up on him? His father stayed, of course, but he was driven to drink by Conner's antics. Died five years ago and did his son bother turning up to his funeral? No, he didn't.'

Flora flew to Conner's defence. 'He's a man now, not a boy. And no one knows what happened in his childhood, Mrs Parker.' He hadn't told anyone.

She paused for a moment, lost in thought as she remembered the love of her own family. Just what had Conner endured? She remembered the day she'd walked along the cliffs to his house.

She remembered the shouting.

'Well, I tell you this much,' Mrs Parker said firmly. 'That boy isn't capable of warmth or sensitivity and he doesn't care about anyone but himself. I still don't believe he's a doctor. He never did a day's studying in his life and as for the way he dresses—well, I mean, Logan's always smart in trousers and a shirt, but Conner hadn't even shaved! He looked—'

Handsome, Flora thought helplessly as she fumbled with the bandage. *He'd looked impossibly, outrageously handsome.*

'Dangerous,' Mrs Parker continued with a shudder, watching as Flora finished the dressing. 'Who in their right minds would trust him with a medical problem? He causes more problems than he solves. Not too tight, dear.'

'It has to be quite tight because we need the pressure on the ankle.'

'I couldn't believe it when I heard Janet booking patients in to see him. I said to Nina Hill, "Well, that's going to be interesting to watch. Now he'll get his comeuppance because no one will see him.'" Having delivered that prediction, Mrs Parker paused expectantly and Flora glanced up at her, realizing that some sort of response was required.

'They'll see him, Mrs Parker,' she said quietly. 'That was then and this is now. Conner is well qualified. And it's great news that Logan finally has help. Super.'

'*Super?*' Mrs Parker gaped at her. 'You think it's great news?'

Far too loyal to reveal her own reservations, Flora secured the bandage. 'Of course. Logan is barely managing on his own. We need another doctor on the island.'

'Well, don't imagine for one moment that Conner MacNeil will make a difference! Even if he *is* a doctor now, which frankly I doubt because everyone knows that these days you can fake everything for a price, there won't be a soul on this island who will trust his opinion.'

Flora took a deep breath and tried to speak. 'Mrs Parker, you really shouldn't—'

'Anyway, enough of that conversation.' Mrs Parker apparently didn't even notice the interruption. 'I refuse to waste the air in my lungs on Conner MacNeil when there are so many more important things going on around us. I meant to say to you, John Carter was seen talking at the school gate with Meg Watson. Now, *that's* an interesting match, if you ask me. She's a single mother and he's…'

Realising that a two-way conversation wasn't required, Flora stood up and washed her hands, only half listening as Mrs Parker regaled her with all the latest island gossip.

How could Conner not be hurt by the negative reaction of the islanders?

Was he really as indifferent as he seemed?

If it were her, she'd be completely mortified.

She tugged a paper towel out of the holder and dried her hands, part of her brain listening to Mrs Parker while the other half thought about Conner. He'd built a shell around himself, and who could blame him?

'So what do you think, dear?'

Realising that this time Mrs Parker was waiting for a response, Flora turned. 'I honestly don't know,' she said truthfully. 'I couldn't give an opinion.' And even if she could, she wouldn't. 'Don't forget it's important to walk when you have a venous ulcer.'

'Yes, yes, I can't possibly forget because you keep telling me.' The elderly lady put her foot on the floor and tested it gingerly. 'Oh, that's much more comfortable. You're a wonderful nurse, dear. Simply wonderful.'

But a useless gossip, Flora thought wryly. 'That's very kind of you, Mrs Parker.'

'Not kind at all. I'm only saying what everyone else is saying.' Angela Parker slipped on her shoes. 'We're all so thrilled that you've come back to the island to take over from our Kyla. Only yesterday I was saying to Meg in the café that we could have ended up with some mainlander with no idea how things work on Glenmore but, no, Dr MacNeil managed to tempt you back. When your father died I thought you might never return but then Nina reminded me that your aunt is here. Did you miss it when you were away?'

Flora felt a sudden shaft of pain as she thought of her father. *She still missed him.* 'Well, I suppose I—'

'Of course you did and now you're back, which is perfect. And Logan has been in desperate need of a practice nurse since Kyla and Dr Walker left, and what with poor Evanna being so pregnant.' Without waiting for Flora to respond, Mrs Parker forged ahead like a ship in a force-nine gale. 'Well, we all know that Dr MacNeil is worried about her, given the tragedy with his first wife. Not that Evanna should have a problem in that direction. She's a girl with good childbearing hips.'

Flora winced and hoped that no one repeated that comment

to her friend and colleague. 'Logan doesn't seem worried,' she lied, 'and Evanna is a midwife, so if anyone understands her condition, she does!'

'Do you really think she should still be working, this close to having that baby?'

Aware that whatever she said would be spread around the island by nightfall, Flora once again kept her answer suitably neutral. 'She isn't on her feet that much. She's just doing the odd morning clinic.' She sat down at her desk and updated the notes on the computer. 'It's fortunate that their house is attached to the surgery. At least she doesn't have to come far to work and I do all the community calls so she doesn't have that to cope with.'

'You see? That's what I mean. It's great that you're back.' Angela Parker picked up her bag and stood up. 'Everywhere I go I hear people saying, "Have you seen our Flora? Doesn't she look well?"'

An intensely private person, Flora felt herself shrink slightly inside. 'People are talking about me?'

'Of course,' Angela said cheerfully. 'A new nurse on Glenmore is big news. People are thrilled. We're all hoping you'll meet a nice young man and then you'll be a permanent fixture on the island. Glenmore is a good place to raise a family, dear.'

A family? 'I think it's a bit soon to be thinking of that,' Flora said faintly, deciding that it was time to end the conversation before gossip about her 'wedding' reached the pub. 'Your leg is healing well, Mrs Parker. Make an appointment to see me again on your way out.'

'Yes, I'll do that. I certainly won't be seeing Conner, that's for sure.' She sniffed. 'I value my health far too much for that.'

Flora opened her mouth to reply and then realised that no reply was expected because Angela Parker was once again answering her own question.

'I think this time Logan will discover he's made a mistake.'

She slid her bag over her arm. 'If he's not careful, he'll find himself handling the summer singlehanded and that won't be an easy task with a toddler and a new bairn.'

Knowing that to comment on that statement would trigger a conversation she didn't have time for, Flora stood up, worried that she'd never finish her clinic if all her patients had as much to say as Angela. 'It was nice to see you. Don't forget to put that leg up when you're sitting down.'

'I always do that.' Angela opened the door. 'Take care of yourself and give me regards to your aunt.'

'I'll do that, Mrs Parker.' Flora waited for the door to close behind her and then sank back into her chair. A quick glance at the clock on the wall confirmed that she was now running *seriously* late and she gave a despairing shake of her head. She still hadn't adjusted to how long each appointment took on Glenmore. Everyone had something to say and a consultation involved so much more than it did on the mainland.

'Problems?' Logan stood in the doorway, a question in his eyes. 'Angela Parker was with you a long time. Is her leg giving her trouble?'

'She still has some signs of eczema around the ulcer but that's because she isn't using the cream you gave her. She's not pyrexial and there's no pain or tenderness to speak of and no obvious signs of cellulitis or infection. I'll keep an eye on it. If it isn't looking any better next week, I'll give you a shout.'

Logan walked into the room and closed the door behind him. 'If there's no sign of healing in another month or so, I'll refer her for a biopsy. We need to exclude malignancy.'

'I think it is healing, it's just that she doesn't do much to help it along.'

'So why are you looking so worried? I can't believe that Mrs Parker's leg ulcer is responsible for that frown on your face.'

'I'm hopeless at this job,' Flora confessed simply. 'Absolutely hopeless.'

'That's utter nonsense.' It was Logan's turn to frown. 'You're a brilliant nurse.'

'It's not the nursing that worries me, it's the rest of it. The gossip, the chat, the rumour machine.' Flora waved a hand in a gesture of despair. 'I'm just no good at it. I've never been any good at just chatting. When I did the clinic in Edinburgh, patients just wanted me to dress their leg or take their blood. On Glenmore, I'm supposed to have an opinion on everything from the Carpenters' divorce to Janey Smith's speeding fine.' She brushed her hair out of her eyes and shot him a helpless look. 'I don't know how to handle it. I don't want to join in, I have no intention of revealing confidential information, but I don't want to look rude. How do you do it? How do you cope?'

'I say "That's interesting" a hundred times a day and if they're really rambling on I adopt my "this could be something serious" look and that soon focuses their minds back on their medical problem. The skill is to cut them off tactfully.'

'I definitely need to work on that skill,' Flora muttered. 'And I confess that I *hate* the idea that everyone is talking about me.'

'This is Glenmore,' Logan said easily. 'Of course people are talking about you. They're talking about everyone. But it's mostly friendly talk. People care and that's what makes this island so special. You've been in the city for too long. You've forgotten what island living is all about. You'll adjust.'

'But the talk isn't friendly about Conner, is it?' Troubled, Flora looked at him. 'They're being horrid to him. I mean, I know I was shocked to see him and even more shocked to discover that he's a doctor, but boycotting his surgery…'

'Some of the patients saw him and word will spread.' Logan smiled. 'Providing he isn't too outrageous. Don't worry about Conner. He can look after himself.'

'Maybe.' She suddenly noticed the dark shadows underneath his eyes. 'You look really, really tired, Logan. Is there anything I can do to help?'

'You're already doing it. Being tired is part of the job description when you work here, as you're fast discovering.' He rubbed his fingers over his forehead. 'And on top of that I was up in the night with little Helen Peters because she—'

'Had a nasty asthma attack,' Flora finished his sentence with a laugh, 'and before you ask, the reason I know is because Mrs Abbott mentioned it when she came in to have her ears syringed and *she* heard it from Sam when she was buying fish on the queue this morning and Sam knew because—'

'He lives across the road from the Peters' sister.' Logan looked amused. 'Relax, Flora. This is how things work on Glenmore. Don't knock it. Sam was the one who called me because there were lights on all over the house and he went across the road to see if he could help.'

Flora's eyes softened. 'That was kind.'

'People are kind here. Don't worry—you'll soon get back into the swing of it. And they'll get used to Conner.'

'I hope you're right. So what happened to little Helen? Did you change her medication?'

'No, but I talked to her mum about exercise.' He frowned. 'It was sports day yesterday. I'm confident that the physical exertion is what triggered it. Any chance that you could you pop in and see them today? It was pretty scary for everyone and I think they'd appreciate an extra dose of reassurance. You might want to have a conversation about lifestyle.'

'I'll pop in, no problem.' This was the Glenmore she knew and loved. Where else would the medical team find time for that sort of visit? That level of care and attention was what made the island special. And she was doing the job she'd been trained to do. Feeling more relaxed, Flora added Helen's name to her list of afternoon calls.

'I'll see you later.' Logan opened the door to leave and Conner strolled in.

Flora's world tilted and her insides knotted with an almost unbearable tension. 'Conner.'

He stepped aside to let Logan pass. 'Isn't Angela Parker a little old to be training for the Olympics? She took one look at me and ran as if the hounds of hell were after her. What's the matter with her leg?'

'Venous ulcer. She's supposed to be mobilising but she doesn't do enough of it.'

'Then perhaps I should stand behind her more often. She ran so fast I could have entered her in the Derby.'

He was so confident, so easy with a situation that most people would have found agonisingly awkward. He really didn't seem to care that the locals had been distinctly unwelcoming. *But if he'd cared, he wouldn't be the man he was.*

Flora cleared her throat. 'Mrs Parker was a little surprised to discover that you're now a doctor.'

Conner smiled. 'Sweet Flora, always coating the truth with honey. Come on, angel. Tell me what she said. The truth. It will be good for you. And my shoulders are broad. I can take it.'

She knew his shoulders were broad—in fact, she was far, far too conscious of his body.

'She doesn't believe you're a doctor and she values her health too much to see you.'

'And I value my sanity far too much to see her, so both of us are happy. If her health is that good, she doesn't need a doctor anyway. So I'm spared.'

'It's not funny.' Ignoring the amusement in his eyes, Flora kept her head down and put a box of vaccine back in the fridge. 'You have no idea what things are like here! We're overwhelmed with work and every day the ferry brings more tourists. Logan needs help. He's barely had time to see his wife and daughter since Ethan left and the baby is due in a few weeks. He needs someone he can trust.'

'And you think he can't trust me?'

'I don't think that's relevant.' Desperate to make him understand, she turned to face him. 'If the patients won't see you, then it doesn't matter what Logan thinks.'

'Relax. The tourists will see me. I'll talk to Janet and make sure she allocates me a surgery full of patients who know nothing about my wicked past.'

'Conner—'

'I wasn't expecting a hero's welcome, Flora.' He gave a faint smile. 'And now you'll have to excuse me. There's a bit of a rush on. Patients are fighting to see me and I don't want to disappoint them.'

Her heart bumped against her chest and she didn't understand it. She couldn't possibly find him attractive. It was ridiculous to find him attractive. *So why were her legs shaking so much she needed to sit down?*

CHAPTER FOUR

'GLENMORE is in an uproar. Eight patients refused to see him this morning and insisted on waiting for Logan.' In the café near the harbour, Flora leaned across the table and helped herself to one of Evanna's sandwiches. 'These are delicious. Why aren't you eating them?'

'Because there's no room in my body for anything except the baby.' Evanna shifted in her seat, obviously uncomfortable. 'They refused to see him? Really? Oh, poor Conner, that's dreadful. Were his feelings hurt, do you think?'

'Does he have feelings?' Flora glanced out of the window, watching idly as groups of tourists walked from the ferry towards the beach. 'Since when did Conner MacNeil care what people think of him? He is Mr Tough Guy.'

'Deep down, I'm sure he cares.'

'If he cared he wouldn't have done his surgery wearing black leather and half an inch of stubble.' Flora winced as a toddler tripped over a fishing rod and fell hard onto the pavement. She watched the mother scoop up the child and offer comfort. 'Believe me, he has no intention of modifying his behaviour to please anyone. He was as defiant and confrontational as ever.' *And sexy. Indecently sexy.*

'If he didn't care, he'd be living in his parents' old house up on the cliffs.'

Flora was silent for a moment. She hadn't given any thought to where Conner was living. 'And he's not?'

'Logan gave him the barn.'

'I thought it was let for the summer.'

'It is. To Conner. When Logan thought he might be coming back, he kept it free for him. I suppose he knew Connor wouldn't want to stay in his parents' house.' Evanna shrugged. 'Who can blame him? I don't suppose it has any nice memories for him. By all accounts, he had a pretty miserable childhood.'

'Then why didn't he sell it after his father died?'

'He hasn't been here to sell it. Perhaps he'll deal with it this summer.'

'Break his final tie with the island? Do you think that's why he's come back? To sell the house?'

'I wouldn't think so. He could have done that with one call to the island estate agent. Perhaps he's laying old ghosts.' Evanna gave a suggestive smile. 'Or maybe he's laying old girl-friends.'

'Evanna!' Struggling between shock and laughter, Flora sent a weak, apologetic smile towards the tourists eating lunch at the next table. 'If you're going to make obscene comments, lower your voice. We still have to work here after Conner's gone.'

'And life will be considerably more boring.'

'Pregnancy has driven you mad.'

'You might be right.' Evanna shifted in her seat. 'I can't remember what it's like not to be fat and exhausted.'

'I think Conner is trying to shock them on purpose. I suspect he wants to provoke a reaction from them.' Flora looked at her and smiled. 'Do you want to know something funny?'

'Not too funny.' Evanna patted her enormous bump gently. 'I have to be economical with laughter at the moment. Go on.'

'Mrs Ellis saw him.'

'As a patient? You're joking.'

'I'm not. I expected her to walk straight back out and call

the police, but she was in there for ages and she came out smiling.'

'So he even charmed her.' Evanna sighed wistfully. 'You see? It doesn't matter how badly he behaves, women just can't help themselves. It's the danger, I suppose. The fact that he's a bit volatile and unstable just adds to his appeal. If you had a date with Conner you never quite knew whether you were going to end up in bed or in a jail cell.'

Flora gasped. 'What exactly do you know about dates with Conner? There is no way your parents would have allowed you anywhere near him.'

'Didn't stop me dreaming.' Evanna sipped her tea. 'I had fantasies, just like you.'

'I did not have fantasies.'

'Now you're lying.' Evanna grinned placidly. 'Every woman dreams about the local bad boy.'

'Conner is well educated.'

'Which makes him all the more attractive,' Evanna sighed.

'My idea of a perfect date never involved a close encounter with the police,' Flora said lightly, 'and I don't believe yours did either. You were always crazy about Logan.'

'That didn't stop me looking. I suppose that's part of the reason Conner was so attractive,' Evanna said simply. 'He was forbidden. Are you seriously telling me you've never had a few fantasies about Conner?'

'Never.' Keen to end what was increasingly becoming an uncomfortable conversation, Flora finished her sandwich and glanced at her watch. 'I have to go. Little Helen Peters had an asthma attack in the night. I'm going to call on her on my way back to the surgery.'

Evanna yawned. 'Yes. Poor Logan was up and down in the night. First it was Helen, then it was our Kirsty.'

'How is she?'

'We've moved her from a cot to a bed in preparation for the arrival of her sibling.' Evanna patted her swollen abdomen gently. 'And she's just discovered that she can leap out whenever she likes and come in with us. Which is fine, except she sleeps like a starfish, arms and legs stuck out at angles designed to cause maximum discomfort to those sharing the space.'

Flora laughed. 'She's gorgeous. Who is looking after her today?'

'Meg had her this morning and I'm going home right now.' Evanna stood up and winced. 'I can't believe this is how it feels to be thirty-five weeks pregnant. Remind me to be more sympathetic next time I run the antenatal clinic. Give little Helen a kiss from me.'

'I will. Why didn't you tell me that Logan had appointed Conner as the doctor?'

'Neither of us were sure he'd turn up. It didn't seem worth mentioning until we knew for sure.'

'So you really don't know why he's back, Evanna?' Flora tried to keep her tone casual.

'No. Logan hasn't said any more to me than he has to you.'

Flora reached for her bag. 'No pillow talk?'

'Are you kidding? Our pillow talk revolves around me telling him how uncomfortable I am and him trying not to phone for an air ambulance.'

'Is he that nervous?'

'He's hiding it quite well but, yes, he's nervous. Of course. His first wife died in childbirth and none of us are likely to forget that, myself included.' Evanna breathed out heavily. 'He wants me to go and stay on the mainland, but the baby's not due for another five weeks and if it was two weeks late I could be stuck over there for seven weeks. Even if I wanted to, which I don't, it just isn't practical. There's Kirsty to think of. I don't want her unsettled.'

'No. Well…' Flora leaned forward and gave her friend a hug, carefully avoiding her bump. 'We're all keeping an eye

on you and we can get you over to the mainland at the first sign
of movement.'

'That's the plan.' Evanna stroked her bump. 'Just hope the
baby is listening.'

Flora drove with the windows down, humming to herself and
enjoying the breeze and the sunshine. She loved Glenmore at
this time of year. Wild flowers clustered on the banks of grass
at the side of the road and in the distance she could see the
jagged silhouette of the ruined castle.

She waved at Doug MacDonald who was out on his bike
and then caught sight of Sonia Davies pushing a buggy on the
pavement.

'Sonia!' She slowed to a halt and called out to the young
mother. 'Everything OK? How's Rachel?'

'She's beautiful.' Sonia pushed the buggy over to the car.
'I'm due in clinic later this week for another immunisation.'

Flora nodded. 'She's twelve months, isn't she? So that will
be the Hib booster. *Haemophilus influenzae.*'

Sonia handed Rachel a rattle to play with. 'I hope she
doesn't freak out. It's different when they're babies, isn't it?
They don't know what's happening and it's over in a flash.'

'She'll be fine. Have you booked her in for Thursday afternoon?'

'Yes.' Sonia jiggled the pushchair. 'No sign of Evanna
having the baby yet, then?'

'She has a few weeks to go yet.'

'I bet Dr MacNeil is nervous.' Sonia gave a little frown. 'We
all know how uneasy he gets when women get near their due
date. When he had to deliver me on the island last year, he was
horrified. Never saw him look nervous before that night. I still
think that if Evanna hadn't been there, he would have done a
runner.'

'I'm sure he wouldn't, although we all know that he prefers
babies to be born on the mainland. I'm sure he'll be packing

Evanna off on that ferry in good time. And I'd better go. I have a visit to do before my afternoon clinic.' Flora slid back into her car. 'See you later in the week, Sonia.'

She carried on up the coast road, called in on Helen to check on her and offer reassurance to her mother. Then she drove to the medical centre, parking next to a sleek black motorbike.

She gave a faint smile. That explained the black leather. A motorbike.

She couldn't imagine Conner with anything else. He was a man who always chose to live his life on the wrong side of risk.

Janet was at the reception desk, trying to find an appointment for a patient. 'Flora has had a cancellation so she can see him straight away, Mrs Gregg,' she was saying. 'I'll put you in with her. If she thinks Harry should see a doctor urgently, she'll arrange it.'

Looking anxious, Mrs Gregg took Harry by the hand and led him to the chairs in the waiting room.

Flora walked up to the desk. 'Problems?'

'Just the one problem. People don't want to book in with Conner.' Janet sighed and rubbed her fingers over her forehead. 'I can't believe that Logan has done this to us in the middle of summer. His afternoon surgery is bursting at the seams and how many does Conner have? Two people.'

'Two? That's all?'

'No one wants to see him, Flora.' Janet looked exhausted. 'I'm sure he's a very good doctor, but all anyone round here remembers is a boy with a lot of problems. They don't trust him.'

Remembering what Logan had said to her, Flora straightened her shoulders. 'His qualifications are excellent.'

'Well, maybe he'd like to put them above my desk in neon lights.'

'It's only his first day. People will settle down,' Flora said firmly, hoping that she was right. 'I thought the women, at least, would be queuing up.'

'I'm sure they will, but not for his medical skills,' Janet said dryly. 'If Logan was looking for help, I think he was looking in the wrong place. Anyway, the Greggs are back from holiday and Harry isn't well. He has a rash and Diane is worried. Your first patient has cancelled so I've put them in with you. If you're worried, perhaps you can persuade them to see Conner, but I don't hold out much hope.'

'Leave it with me. If you see Logan can you tell him that I popped in to see Helen and she was fine?' Flora walked to the waiting area. Harry was sitting on his mother's lap and his eyes were closed.

'Hello, Nurse Harris.' Diane gave her a tired smile. 'Janet said you might fit us in.'

'Of course.' Flora touched the little boy's forehead with a gentle hand. 'He's very hot.'

'I've spent the past two nights trying to bring his temperature down.' Diane clearly hadn't slept for days and her face was pale and drawn. 'But it's the rash that's really worrying me. It's spreading.'

'I'll take a look.'

The woman gave her a grateful smile and gently eased Harry onto the floor. 'You're too big for Mummy to carry now,' she murmured, taking his hand. 'Just walk as far as the consulting room, then you can sit down again.'

Harry murmured a protest but trotted along the corridor towards Flora's consulting room.

'Tell me what happened. I'd like to know when Harry first became ill.' Flora flicked on her computer and stowed her bag under the desk. 'Presumably it started on holiday?'

'Three days ago he developed this rash. One minute he was fine and the next he had a temperature, neck stiffness, headache.' Diane swallowed. 'He's gone from well to ill really fast and that's— Well, I'm worried.'

Understanding that she didn't want to say too much in front of the child, Flora nodded. 'And you think the rash has spread?'

'Oh, yes. Definitely.'

Flora washed her hands. 'I'll take a look, if that's all right.'

'I'm just going to take your T-shirt off, Harry.' Diane reached forward and lifted his T-shirt carefully over his head. 'I want to show Nurse Harris.'

Harry gave a moan of protest. 'I'm really, really cold.'

'That's because you have a temperature,' Flora said gently, lifting his arm slightly and turning him towards the light. 'When did you first notice the rash, Mrs Gregg?'

'Well, it didn't look like this at first. It started with just one red spot under his arm and then it spread. Then his temperature shot up and he's been feeling boiling hot ever since.' Diane pushed her son's hair away from his face and touched his forehead. 'He's hot now.'

Flora examined the rash carefully. It was scarlet and circular and she'd never seen anything like it before. 'Did you see a doctor when you were away?'

'Yes, but he said it was just a virus.' Diane rolled her eyes, her worry evident. 'Perhaps it is, but I wanted a proper opinion. It isn't until you leave Glenmore that you realise how good the medical care is on this island. I was hoping to see Dr MacNeil, but Janet says his surgery is full.'

Flora checked Harry's temperature and recorded it. 'Logan isn't the only doctor working at Glenmore now,' she said carefully, and Diane pursed her lips.

'If you're talking about Conner MacNeil, I'm not interested. I remember the time he set off that firework in the school library.'

'That was a long time ago, Mrs Gregg.' Flora checked Harry's pulse and blood pressure. 'He trained in the army. His qualifications are excellent.'

'I don't care. I—'

'Didn't you ever do anything you shouldn't when you were young?'

'Well, I—I suppose…'

'I know I did.' Flora shrugged. 'And I also know I wouldn't want to be judged as an adult by how I was as a child. People change, Mrs Gregg. And everyone deserves to be given chances. Logan wouldn't have taken Conner on if he didn't trust him. I'd like him to see Harry. I don't recognise this rash and the fact that he has a temperature makes it worth exploring further.'

Mrs Gregg hesitated and then glanced at Harry, clearly torn. 'I don't suppose Conner will know any more than that doctor on the mainland.'

'Let's give it a try—see what he says? I'll see if he's free,' Flora said cheerfully, trying not to reveal that the chances of Conner having a patient with him was extremely remote.

Hoping that she wasn't making a mistake, she went across the corridor and tapped on his door. 'Conner?' She walked in and found him absorbed in a website on the internet. She peered closer. 'Wetsuits?'

'I'm planning to do some sailing. It looks as though I'm going to have plenty of time on my hands.' He swivelled his head and looked at her. 'Are you here to relieve my boredom?'

She flushed. 'I have a patient that needs to be seen by a doctor.'

'And?'

'You're a doctor.'

'Am I?' He lounged back in his chair, his ice-blue gaze disturbingly direct. 'So why am I sitting in an empty consulting room?'

'Because this is Glenmore and it takes folks a while to get used to change. The last time they saw you, you were stirring up trouble all over the island. I don't suppose anyone imagined you'd become a doctor. So will you see Harry Gregg?'

Conner's eyes narrowed. 'Diane's son?'

'Yes. He's eight years old and a really nice little boy. Very lively usually, but not today. Diane is frightened.'

'She always did have a tendency to overreact. I remember she slapped my face once.'

'You probably deserved it.'

He smiled. 'I probably did. So what do you think, Flora? Paranoid mother?'

Flora shook her head. 'I think it's something that needs looking at. The child is poorly, there's no doubt about that. And he has a really weird rash. I've never seen anything like it before.'

Conner rose to his feet. 'Is she going to slap my face again or run away screaming in horror if I walk into the room?'

'I've no idea.' Flora gave a weary smile. 'Let's try it, shall we? Harry needs to see a doctor and I'd rather it was sooner than later.'

Diane looked up as they walked into the room. 'Dr MacNeil.'

'Diane.' Conner's greeting was cursory, his eyes focused on the boy, who was now sitting on his mother's lap, his head on her chest. 'Hey, sport.' He hunkered down so that he was on the same level. 'What's going on with you?'

Harry opened his eyes but didn't move his head. 'Feel bad.'

'His temperature is thirty-nine degrees.' Flora gently lifted Harry's arm so that Conner could see. 'He's had this rash for three days.'

'Feel horrible,' the boy muttered, and Conner nodded.

'Well, we need to see what we can do about that.' He studied the rash in silence, his blue eyes narrowed slightly. 'Circular rash.'

Diane watched his face. 'You're going to tell me that it's just a virus and that I shouldn't have bothered you.'

Conner lifted his gaze to hers. 'You were right to bring him. Harry? Do you mind undressing down to your underpants? I want to take a proper look at this rash.'

Flora helped the child undress and Conner examined his skin carefully and questioned Diane in detail.

'It started under his arm when we were on holiday,' she told him. 'Just a red spot. And then it grew bigger and it turned into that weird thing he has now.'

'Where did you go on holiday?'

Flora glanced at him in surprise. She wouldn't have expected Conner to be interested in small talk.

'Mainland.'

'Highlands?' Conner ran a finger over the rash, his expression thoughtful. 'Were you walking?'

'Yes.' Diane looked at him. 'How do you know?'

Conner straightened and reached for Harry's T-shirt. 'It fits with what I'm seeing. You can get dressed now. I've seen all I need to see.' He gently pulled the T-shirt over the boy's head. 'Were you camping?'

'Yes. We spent a few nights in a forest. It was lovely.'

'Lots of deer around?'

'Actually, yes.' Diane frowned. 'How do you know that?'

'Because Harry has Lyme disease.' Conner washed his hands. 'He was almost certainly bitten by a tick, which is why he started off with one red spot. Did you see an insect?'

'No.' Bemused, Diane shook her head. 'No, I didn't. But we've been camping every year since he was born and we've never had a problem. Lyme disease? What is that? I've never even heard of it.'

'It's not that common in this country, although the number of cases is increasing. Ticks are tiny insects and they feed by sucking blood from animals such as deer. Some ticks get infected with the bacterium that causes Lyme disease and if they bite a human then they pass the disease on.'

Diane looked at him in a mixture of horror and amazement. 'And you're sure Harry has it? How do you know?'

'Because his symptoms fit the history.'

Flora felt the tension leave her. Clearly Conner hadn't been making small talk about holidays, he'd been verifying the cause of the symptoms he was seeing. Logan was right. Conner was a good doctor. *A clever doctor.* And Diane appeared to have forgotten that she'd ever had reservations about seeing him.

'You've seen this Lyme disease before?'

'When I was stationed overseas.' Without waiting for an invitation, he sat down at Flora's computer and hit a few keys, bringing up a list of antibiotics. 'The rash that Harry has is fairly typical.' He scrolled down, searching for the one he wanted. 'It starts as a single circular red mark and it gradually spreads. It isn't always painful or itchy and some people don't even notice it, depending on where they were bitten.'

'Is there any treatment?'

'Yes.' Conner's eyes were fixed on the screen. 'I'm going to give Harry some antibiotics.'

'And will they work?'

'They should do because we've caught it early. You did the right thing, bringing him in.'

'The doctor on the mainland thought it was a virus.' Diane's mouth tightened with disapproval. 'Virus is a word doctors use when they haven't got a clue what's going on.'

'You might be right. I usually say "I don't know" but that phrase doesn't win you many friends either. In fairness to your guy on the mainland, Lyme disease is not a condition every doctor will have seen.' Conner printed off the prescription and handed it to Diane. 'Make sure Harry finishes the course.'

'I'll do that.' She slipped the prescription into her bag and hesitated. 'Thank you.' She looked Conner in the eye. 'I wasn't sure about seeing you…'

'I don't blame you for that.' As cool as ever, Conner rose to his feet. 'Make an appointment to see Logan in a few days. Harry needs to be followed up. We need to be sure that the antibiotics are working.'

Diane took Harry's hand in hers. 'Why should I see Logan? Are you going to be busy?'

Conner gave a faint smile. 'On current form? Probably not. But it's important that the patients have faith in the doctor they see.'

'I agree.' Diane walked towards the door. 'Which is why we'll be making that appointment when you're doing surgery.

Thank you, Dr MacNeil. I knew I could rely on a Glenmore doctor to get the diagnosis right.' The door closed behind her and Flora smiled happily at Conner.

'I think you're a hit. That was pretty impressive. I predict that once word spreads, your surgery will be crammed with patients.'

'And I'm supposed to rejoice about that?'

'Maybe not. But Logan will. So, tell me about Lyme disease because I'm feeling horribly ignorant.'

'What else do you want to know? You get bitten by a tick that clings on once it bites. Then it sucks your blood—'

'Don't!' Flora pulled a face. 'You're telling it like a horror story. If you carry on like that I'll never set foot outside again.'

It was the wrong thing to say to Conner. He leaned against the desk and gave a wicked smile. 'As I was saying, they suck your blood and slowly become more and more engorged—'

'You do it on purpose, don't you? Try and shock people.'

'I admit it's an extremely stimulating pastime.'

'You might not find it so funny when I'm sick,' Flora said sweetly, and his smile widened.

'Nurses aren't supposed to have delicate constitutions.'

'Doctors aren't supposed to be bloodthirsty.'

'I'm just delivering the facts.'

'Well…' She was horribly aware of just how strong his shoulders were and how much he dominated her tiny room. 'Could you deliver them with slightly less gruesome relish?'

'Where was I?' He angled his head slightly. 'Oh, yes, they were engorged with blood. Anyway, the bacteria that cause Lyme disease are usually carried in the gut and only travel to their mouth once they've been feeding for about twenty-four hours. So if you remove the tick as soon as you're bitten, you're unlikely to be infected.'

Flora shuddered. 'So you're telling me that a method of prevention is to drag this greedy, engorged creature off your skin?'

'You remove it before it's engorged. And you don't drag. If you drag, you'll just leave the mouth stuck in your body.'

'Enough!'

'The best thing is to smother it with Vaseline. It suffocates and then you can remove it with a pair of tweezers. You shouldn't use your fingers—'

'I wouldn't touch it with a bargepole! And I'm never venturing outside again without full protective clothing.'

Conner's eyes flickered to the neck of her uniform. 'You don't need to overdo it. The tick that carries the bacteria likes areas where there are wild deer.'

Her heart started to beat just a little bit faster. 'And that's why you were so interested in where the Greggs went on holiday?'

'The symptoms fitted. The fact that they'd been camping in a forest in warm weather made it highly possible that he'd contracted the disease. Ticks like warm weather and people wear less then so they're more likely to be bitten.' His eyes lifted to hers and the tension between them increased.

'Why haven't I heard of it?'

'Obviously there haven't been any cases on Glenmore. It's sensible to take precautions if you're walking or camping in an area where infected ticks are known to live.' His eyes dropped to her mouth, his gaze lingering. 'Wear long sleeves and trousers, use a tick repellent spray—all the obvious things.'

They were talking about medical matters and yet there was a sudden intimacy in the atmosphere that she didn't understand. It circled her like a forcefield, drawing her in, and when the phone rang suddenly she gave a start.

He was between her and the desk and she waited for him to move to one side so that she could answer it, but he stayed where he was. Left with no choice, she was forced to brush past him as she reached for the receiver. 'Yes? I mean…' Flustered by the fact that he was standing so close to her, she stumbled over the words. 'Nurse Harris speaking— Oh, hello, Mr

Murray.' Struggling to concentrate, she listened as the man on the other end spoke to her. 'Well, no, I hadn't heard of it either, but—' She broke off and listened again before finally shaking her head. 'You'd better speak to him yourself.'

She sighed and handed the receiver to Conner. 'It's Mr Murray, the pharmacist down on South Quay. He has a question about the prescription you just gave Harry.'

Relaxed and confident, Conner took the phone from her, his gaze still locked with hers. 'MacNeil.'

Flora felt as though someone had lit a fire inside her body. She should look away. She knew she should look away but she just couldn't help herself. There was something in his ice-blue eyes that insisted that she look.

'That's right, Mr Murray, the dose is large.' He listened, his eyes still fixed on hers. 'Yes, I do know that I'm not treating a horse.'

Flora frowned and mouthed, 'A horse?' But Conner merely lifted a hand and trailed a finger down her cheek with agonising slowness.

'No, believe it or not, I'm not trying to kill him, Mr Murray,' he drawled softly, his finger lingering near her mouth. 'I'm treating a case of Lyme disease. If you look it up I think you'll find that the dose I've given him is appropriate…Yes, even in a child.' He brushed her lower lip with his thumb as he continued to field a tirade from the island pharmacist. 'Yes, I do remember the incident with the firework. Yes, and the barn— No, I don't blame you for questioning me, Mr Murray.' His hand dropped to his side and she sensed a sudden change in him. 'Of course, you're just doing your job.'

Finally he replaced the receiver. 'Apparently it isn't just the patients who have a problem trusting my judgement.'

His tone was flat and Flora stood still, wanting to say something but not knowing what. 'It was an unusual prescription.'

'You don't need to make excuses for them, Flora.' Conner straightened and walked towards the door, his face expressionless. 'You'd better carry on with your surgery. You have patients lining the waiting room.'

She stared after him as he left the room, wanting to stop him. She wanted to say something that would fix things because she sensed that beneath his bored, devil-may-care attitude there was a seam of pain buried so deep that no one could touch it.

The islanders were wary of him, that was true, but what did he think of them?

Remembering Logan's words, Flora bit her lip. When had anyone given Conner MacNeil a chance? When had anyone given him the benefit of the doubt? Why should he bother with any of them when they'd never bothered with him?

It was going to take more than one or two successful consultations to fill his consulting room with patients because no one believed that Conner MacNeil could be anything but a Bad Boy.

It was going to take a miracle.

CHAPTER FIVE

THE miracle didn't happen.

A few of the locals reluctantly agreed to see Conner, but the majority refused, choosing to wait a week to see Logan rather than be forced to consult the island rebel.

'It's ridiculous,' Flora told Evanna crossly a week after Conner had arrived on Glenmore. They were sitting on a rug on the beach, watching Kirsty dig in the sand. Finally the wind had dropped and the sun shone. 'They tell Janet it's urgent, and then say they'd rather wait than see Conner. I mean, just how urgent can something be if it can wait a week? Frankly, it would serve them right if a bit of them dropped off.'

'Well, to be fair to them, Conner was a bit wild and crazy,' Evanna said mildly, picking up Kirsty's sunhat and putting it back on her head. 'We just need to give them time to realise that he's changed.'

'Time isn't on our side. Glenmore needs another doctor. A doctor the patients will see! Your baby is due in four weeks,' Flora reminded her. 'If the patients don't stop demanding to see Logan, you won't get a look-in.'

Evanna sighed. 'I know. He's shattered. He used to always get home before I put Kirsty to bed. Now I'm lucky if he's home before *I'm* in bed.' She lifted her face to the sun. 'It's hot today.'

'I gather from Logan that your blood result was all right.'

Flora lifted a bottle of water out of her bag and took a sip. 'That's a relief all round.'

'Yes, I was already immune to chickenpox, so that's one less problem to contend with.'

Flora was still pondering the problem of Conner. 'It isn't as if he's a useless doctor. He's brilliant. You should have seen him with Harry Gregg.' She leaned forward and helped Kirsty ease the sand out of the bucket. 'There! A perfect castle.' She smiled as Kirsty clapped her hands with delight. 'And he's diagnosed Mrs Ellis.'

'Yes, she told me he's given her thyroxine. He certainly seems to know what he's doing.'

'So why hasn't word spread? Why won't the islanders see him?'

'Because they see the boy and not the man? I'm guessing, but I suppose they just don't trust him.' Evanna hesitated. 'Apparently Finn Sullivan refused to rent him a yacht a few evenings ago.'

Flora stared at her. 'Are you serious?'

'Yes, but it's not all black. I saw Conner kicking a football around with the kids on the beach yesterday. They think he's *so* cool. And several women have made appointments to see him, but I don't think he was too thrilled about that.'

'He certainly wasn't.' Flora brushed sand from Kirsty's face. 'He strode up to Janet and said, "I'm not a bloody gynaecologist" or something equally unsympathetic. And Janet pointed out that as we didn't have a female doctor, he was expected to see female problems.'

'And what was Conner's response to that?'

'I don't know because he lowered his voice but Janet went scarlet.'

Evanna laughed. 'I don't suppose there was much call for gynecology in the army. According to Logan, he was dealing with a lot of trauma. Anyway, it's time we helped him settle in, which is why I've invited him to join us for lunch later.'

Flora's heart bumped hard against her chest. 'He's coming to lunch? I thought it was just your family. Logan, Meg and a few others.'

'Conner is family. I thought it might be a good idea to remind people of that.'

'Oh.' Flora concentrated on Kirsty. 'Well, that's great. Really nice of you, Evanna. So we should go back to the house. Start getting ready.' She rose to her feet and picked Kirsty up. 'Come on, sweetheart. Let's get the sand off your feet and take you home. Who knows? Your daddy might even be there.'

Conner's feet echoed on the cracked wooden floorboards and he glanced around him, feeling the memories swirl. The house smelled of damp, but that wasn't surprising because it had been years since the light and air had been allowed to pour unrestricted through its doors and windows.

He'd always hated this house and nothing had changed. It was as if the walls had absorbed some of the anger and hatred that had been played out in these rooms.

He tried to feel something positive, but there was nothing that wasn't dark and murky, and he gave a soft curse and strode out of the front door and back into the sunshine, drawing the clear air deep into his lungs.

Just walking into the house had made him feel contaminated.

He shouldn't have come.

He should have just paid someone to sell the damn place.

Beneath him the sea crashed onto the rocks and he sucked in a breath, drinking in the wildness of it—the savage beauty. Everything about this part of Glenmore was angry. The coast, the sea, the wind, the house...

Him?

Conner stood for a moment, battling with uncomfortable thoughts until some inner sense warned him that he wasn't alone.

He turned swiftly and saw her.

Flora was standing only metres away from him, the wind lifting her brown curls and blowing them around her face, her expression uncertain.

'Sorry.' Her voice faltered and it was obvious that she couldn't decide whether to stay or retreat. 'I didn't mean to disturb you.'

He wished she hadn't, because he was in no mood for company and his desperate need for isolation fuelled his temper. 'Then why did you?'

Flora flinched at his directness, but she didn't retreat. 'You were supposed to be at Logan and Evanna's for lunch. We assumed you'd forgotten.'

'I needed some space.'

'Oh.' She took a breath. 'It's just that…you didn't ring or anything.'

'No.'

'I was worried.'

'Why?' *Since when had anyone worried about him?*

'This business with the islanders,' she shrugged, embarrassed and awkward. 'It's horrible. I thought by now they would have accepted you.'

'It's not important.'

'Of course it's important! Evanna told me that Finn wouldn't rent you a boat—'

When he didn't answer, she gazed at him in exasperation. 'Don't you *care*?'

He could feel the blood throbbing in his veins. 'What are you doing here, Flora?'

'When you didn't show up, I thought I'd bring lunch to you.'

It was then that he noticed the basket by her feet. He could see a bowl of strawberries, thick whipped cream and another bowl, this one piled high with bronzed chicken legs. And white and red checked napkins.

A traditional picnic.

It was all so civilised and in such direct contrast to this place and everything he was feeling that he felt his tension levels soar.

He wasn't feeling civilised. He wasn't feeling civilised at all.

In fact, he was in an extremely dangerous mood.

'It's pretty here,' she ventured hesitantly, glancing over to the rocks and the tiny beach. 'This is the only house on the island that has its own private beach.'

'Flora, if you have any sense, you'll leave right now.'

Her eyes flew to his. Widened. 'I've made you angry.'

There was something different about her but he couldn't work out what it was. 'I was angry before you arrived. I know you mean well, but I don't wish to take a trip down memory lane and I especially don't want to do it holding anyone's hand,' he said harshly. 'How did you know where to find me?'

'I went to your barn first and you weren't there.' She captured a strand of hair as it danced in the breeze. 'And I saw Mrs North picking blackberries in the lane outside and she said she'd seen you coming in this direction.'

Conner's mood darkened still further. 'Now I know why they don't bother with CCTV on Glenmore. They have locals stationed on every street corner.'

'I shouldn't have come. I really am sorry.' Flushed and flustered, Flora lifted the basket and stepped forward. She pushed the basket into his hands, her smile brief and shy. 'Take it. Evanna is an amazing cook. Her chicken is delicious and the strawberries are freshly picked from the Roberts' farm. If you're not hungry now, you can eat it later.' Without waiting for him to reply, she turned and walked quickly away from him, her long flowery skirt swirling around her body, outlining the soft curve of her hips.

He'd offended her. *Or had he frightened her?*

Conner watched her for a moment and then looked down at the basket and swore long and fluently. The day was *not* turning out as he'd planned. He lifted his gaze from the strawberries and stared after her retreating figure with a mixture of exasperation and anger.

He didn't care that he'd offended her.

He really didn't care.

It wasn't as if he'd invited her here. He hadn't asked her to follow him.

Caught in an internal battle, he opened his mouth to speak, changed his mind and closed it again, then growled with frustration and called out to her. 'Do you like strawberries?'

She stopped and turned—slowly. 'Yes. I love them.'

But she didn't move and even from this distance Conner sensed her wariness and remembered what Logan had said about her being shy.

'Good. Because there's a large bowlful in this basket and I hate them.' He dumped the basket on the ground and looked at her expectantly, but she still didn't move.

'Just eat the chicken, then.'

Realising that she wasn't going to walk to him, he strolled towards her and suddenly saw what was different about her. 'You're not wearing your glasses.'

She lifted a hand to her cheek and shrugged self-consciously. 'Contact lenses. I don't usually wear them at work. I'm not a morning person and I'm never awake enough to risk putting my fingers into my eyes.' She looked over his shoulder at the basket, which now lay abandoned on the soft grass. 'I can take the strawberries with me, if they offend you that much.'

'Or you can sit down and eat them here.'

Her eyes narrowed. 'I didn't think you were looking for company.'

'If the strawberries aren't eaten, I'll hurt Evanna's feelings.'

A smile touched her mouth. 'I thought you didn't care about other people's feelings, Conner MacNeil.'

'I don't, but if I upset her, Logan will give me a black eye.

And then the locals will think I've seduced someone's wife or girlfriend. And I'm already in enough trouble.'

She laughed, as he'd intended. 'You told me that you thrive on trouble.'

'That's just habit. I've never known anything else.'

Her laughter faded and she stared up into his face. 'I shouldn't have come here. It's personal for you. Stressful. And you don't want to talk about it, do you?'

He gave a twisted smile. 'Let's just say that if I talk, you wouldn't like the language I'd choose to use.'

'Use whatever language you please. I'm not as shockable as you seem to think I am.'

'It would be all too easy to shock you, Flora.' He thought of what his life had been and then he looked down at her gentle eyes and her soft mouth and wondered why he'd stopped her walking away. 'I'm not the type of man who eats strawberries with girls in flowered skirts.'

'You don't like my skirt?'

'You look…' He gave a faint smile as he searched for the word that best described her. 'Wholesome. Like an advert for that whipped cream in the basket.'

'It's Evanna's whipped cream. And I don't see what my skirt has to do with anything. Do you always push people away?'

'I don't have to. They usually run all by themselves.'

'Well, I can't run in these shoes.'

'Is that right? In that case, you can sit down and help me eat this damn picnic.'

'Where?' Flora glanced towards the house and he made an impatient sound.

'No way.' *He wasn't going back in there.* Instead, he took her hand, scooped up the basket and then led her down the path to the tiny cove at the bottom. The path was steep and stony but she didn't falter, confident and sure-footed despite her comment about her shoes.

She was a local girl, he remembered. *She'd spent her child-*

hood playing on these cliffs and exploring Glenmore's rocky shores.

As they reached the sand, she slipped off her shoes and stooped to pick them up. 'It's pretty here. Really sheltered.'

'Haven't you been here before?'

'No.'

'Why not?'

'Honestly?' She hesitated. 'This beach is part of your property and we were too afraid of your father. Even Kyla.'

Conner gave a bitter laugh. 'Lovely man, my father.' He sat down on the sand and then glanced at her with a frown. 'Did you bring something to sit on?'

She smiled and sat down on the sand next to him. 'This is perfect.' She reached into the basket and then glanced at him, her eyes twinkling. 'Napkin?'

'Of course,' he said sarcastically. 'I'd hate to drop anything on my tuxedo.'

She laughed and passed him the bowl of chicken instead. 'Try this. I guarantee it will taste better than anything you've ever eaten before, tuxedo or no tuxedo. I bumped into Diane Gregg in the supermarket this morning. She said Harry is feeling much better.'

'Yes. I saw him in surgery yesterday. One of the advantages of being treated like a leper is that I have plenty of time for the patients that do want to see me.' He bit into the chicken and flavours exploded on his palate. 'You're right—this is good.'

'I have a boat, if you want to sail.'

Conner lifted an eyebrow. 'Are you making a pass at me?'

The colour poured into her cheeks. 'Of course not.'

'But you're offering to lend me your boat?'

'Yes.' She delved into the basket and pulled out some crusty bread. 'Or we could sail together. You can sail it singlehanded but it's more fun with two.'

'I didn't know you sailed.'

'I suspect there's quite a lot about me that you don't know,' she said calmly, and Conner gave a surprised laugh.

'And what do you think the locals will say when they see you consorting with Bad Conner?'

Flora broke the bread in two and handed him half. 'I suppose it might be sensible to avoid getting into trouble, just in case the lifeboat crew refuse to help.'

'You'd be all right. They'd pick you up and leave me in the water.'

'No problems, then. Lemonade?'

Conner winced. 'Are you serious? What is this—nursery food?'

'It's home-made. Evanna makes it.' She poured him a glass and he heard a dull clunk as ice cubes thudded into the glass. 'It's very refreshing.'

He took the glass and stared at it dubiously. 'If you say so.'

'You'd probably prefer beer.'

'I don't drink.' He felt her eyes on his face and when she spoke her voice was soft.

'Because of your father.' Her quiet statement required no response and so he didn't give one.

They ate in silence and he found himself glancing at her occasionally and noticing things about the way she looked. Like the fact that she had tiny freckles on her nose and that her eyes were incredibly pretty.

'You should ditch the glasses,' he said softly, and she blinked awkwardly.

'Oh…' She concentrated on the chicken and suddenly he was reminded of a baby kitten he'd found abandoned when he'd been a child. It had been so soft and vulnerable that he he'd been afraid to touch it in case he harmed it. So he'd placed an anonymous call to the vet's surgery and had then hidden behind a tree, watching until they'd picked it up.

Flora had that same air of vulnerability.

They finished the picnic in silence and she packed everything away tidily in the basket. 'There's a good wind. I always find there's nothing better than sailing to clear the mind and put everything into perspective.'

'Flora—'

'Don't pretend you don't want to sail, because I know you tried to hire a boat from Finn at the sailing school. I'm offering you my boat. With or without myself as crew.'

He stared out to sea. 'I was going to clear the house out this afternoon.'

'There's no worse job in the world,' she said softly. 'After Dad died, it took me six months to even go into the house. I just couldn't face all those memories. And mine were happy ones. Are you sure you don't want to talk about this?'

'I wouldn't know what to say. I've been away for twelve years. But it seems even that isn't long enough.' Conner took a mouthful of his drink and choked. 'That is truly disgusting.'

Flora laughed. 'Some people prefer it with sugar.'

'The only way I'd drink it is topped up with gin. And given that I don't touch alcohol, there's no chance of that.' Pulling a face, he emptied his glass onto the sand. 'Where's your boat moored?'

'South Quay.'

His eyes narrowed. 'In full public view.'

'Yes.' She scrambled to her feet and brushed the sand from her skirt. 'We need to go via my house so that I can change, but that will only take a minute.'

'You seriously want to sail? I thought you hated being the focus of people's attention.'

'I won't be the focus,' she muttered, carefully stacking everything back into the basket. 'You will.'

She was being kind, he realised. Trying to show solidarity in front of the locals.

He probably ought to refuse but just as he opened his mouth to do just that, the wind gusted and he glanced at the waves breaking on the beach. 'It's a perfect afternoon for a sail.'

'Then what are you waiting for?' She walked towards the path. 'Are you coming, Dr MacNeil? Or would you rather spend the afternoon being moody?'

She'd never had so much fun. The wind was gusting at five knots and Conner was a born sailor, with a natural feel for the wind and the sea and blessed with nerves of steel. And although they came close several times, he didn't land them in the water.

As the water sprayed over the bows, Flora laughed in delight. 'Who taught you to sail?'

'Taught myself. Sank two boats in the process. Probably why Finn won't rent me a boat. I always loved being on the water. The sea was the place where everything came together.' He tightened the mainsheet as he turned the boat into the wind. 'Ready about,' he called. Flora released the jib sheet and they both ducked under the boom as the boat came swiftly around. The wind caught the sails and the boat accelerated smoothly away, the sea sparkling in the summer sunshine.

It was hours before they finally turned the boat back towards the jetty and Flora felt nothing but regret. 'Do you ever feel like just sailing away and never looking back?'

'All the time.' He adjusted the sail. 'What about you?'

'Oh, yes.' She gazed dreamily up at the sky, loving the feel of the wind and the spray on her face. 'I love being on the boat. It's just so easy and comfortable. No people. No problems.'

'You are full of surprises, Flora Harris.' Conner laughed. 'I never imagined you were a sailor.'

'I bought her with the money Dad left me when he died. He was the one who taught me to sail. I was hopeless at team sports at school because I was too shy. No one ever picked me. I think Dad realised that sailing would suit me. I love the freedom of the boat. And the fact that you're away from people.' She closed her eyes and let the sun warm her skin. 'I'm always tense around people.'

'You're still incredibly shy, aren't you?'

She opened her eyes. 'Yes. But I've learned to act. That's what you do as an adult, isn't it? You act your way through situations that would have paralysed you as a child.'

'Was it that bad?'

'Yes.' Her simple, honest response touched him.

'I didn't realise. I just thought you were studious.'

Flora stared at the quay, measuring the distance. 'If I was absorbed in a book then no one bothered with me, and I preferred it that way. I liked being inconspicuous.'

'So why did you come back to Glenmore? Logan said you were working in Edinburgh before this. I would have thought it was easier to be inconspicuous in a city.'

'It's also very lonely and I missed the scenery and the sailing. Coming back here seemed like the right thing to do.'

'And was it?'

She glanced at him. 'I don't know. Even though I know they mean well, I can't get used to the fact that everyone knows what everyone is doing.'

They approached the jetty and she released the jib sheet and the sail flapped in the wind. Conner turned the boat head to wind and brought her skilfully into the quay.

'She's pretty.' He ran a hand over the mast and Flora felt her heart kick against her chest.

She wished she were the boat.

He leapt over the foredeck onto the quay and secured the boat to the jetty while Flora de-rigged the boat, wishing they could have stayed out on the water. Now that they were on dry land she was suddenly aware that she was with Conner MacNeil and that all the locals were watching them.

As usual, Conner was totally indifferent. 'I had no idea your father encouraged you to indulge in such dangerous pastimes. My impression was that he kept you under lock and key. He was strict.'

'Not strict, exactly. Protective.' Flora stepped off the boat and onto the quay. Hot after the exertion, she removed her hat and her hair tumbled loose over her shoulders. 'My mother died when I was very young and I think he was terrified that something would happen to me, too. He never relaxed if I was out.'

'I don't remember you ever going out. All my memories of you have books in them.'

Flora laughed. 'That was partly my fault. I was painfully shy and books stopped me having to talk to people.'

'So why aren't you shy with me, Flora?'

Her eyes flew to his, startled. It was true, she realised. She'd had such fun she hadn't once felt shy with him. Not once. 'I'm never shy when I'm sailing.'

But she knew that it had nothing to do with the sailing and everything to do with the man.

She felt comfortable with Conner.

Unsettled by that thought, she looked across the quay at the throngs of tourists who were milling around on their way to and from the beach. 'Can I treat you to a hot fudge sundae? Meg's café is calorie heaven.'

'I don't think so.' He checked that the boat was securely tied. 'I just upset the balance of Glenmore. I'm like you. Better with the boat than people. I've never been any good at platitudes and all the other false things people say to each other.'

It was so close to the way she felt that for a moment she stood still. Who would have thought that she and Conner had so many similarities? 'But you came back.'

He gave a careless shrug. 'It was time.'

But it wouldn't be for long, she knew that.

Suddenly she just wanted to drag him straight back on the boat and sail back out to sea. On the water she'd had glimpses of the person behind the bad boy. He'd been relaxed. Good-humoured. Now they were back on dry land his ice-blue eyes were wary and cynical, as though he was braced for criticism.

A commotion on the far side of the quay caught her eye and she squinted across the water. 'I wonder why the ferry hasn't left yet.' Flora glanced at her watch. 'It's five past four. Jim always leaves at four o'clock sharp. He's never late.'

'Obviously he is today.'

'What are they all staring at?' An uneasy feeling washed over her. 'Something is happening on the quay. Conner, I think someone must have fallen into the water.'

A woman started screaming hysterically and Flora paled as she recognised her.

'That's Jayne Parsons, from the dental surgery. Something must have happened to Lily. It must be little Lily in the water.' She started to run, dodging groups of gaping tourists as she flew towards the other side of the quay.

And suddenly she could see why people were staring.

Blood pooled on the surface of the water and Flora felt a wave of nausea engulf her as she realised just how serious the situation was.

Her hand shaking, she delved in her pocket for her mobile phone and quickly rang the coastguard and the air ambulance. Then she caught Jayne by the shoulders before she could throw herself into the water after her child. 'No! Wait, Jayne. What happened? Is it Lily?'

'She fell. One minute she was eating her ice cream and the next…Oh, God, she fell.' Jayne's breath was coming in hysterical gasps and out of the corner of her eye Flora saw movement, heard a splash and turned to see Conner already in the water.

A local who had seen the whole incident started directing him. 'She went in about here. Between the quay and the boat. I guess the propeller…' His voice tailed off as he glanced towards Jayne and the woman's eyes widened in horror as she focused on the surface of the water and saw what Flora had already seen.

The blood.

Jayne started to scream and the sound had a thin, inhuman quality that cut through the summer air and brought horrified silence to the normally bustling quay. Then she tried to launch herself into the water again and Flora winced as Jayne's flying fist caught her on the side of her head. She was too slight to hold the woman, her head throbbed and she was just about to resign herself to the fact that Jayne was going to jump when two burly local fishermen came to her aid.

They drew a sobbing, struggling Jayne away from the edge of the quay and Flora gave them a grateful nod. Whatever happened next, Jayne being in the water would only make things worse.

Oblivious to the audience or the building tension, Conner vanished under the water. Time and time again he dived, while strangers and locals stood huddled in groups, watching the drama unfold.

Offering what comfort she could, Flora took Jayne's hand. 'Conner will find her,' she said firmly, praying desperately that she was right. 'Conner will find her.' *If she said it often enough, perhaps it would happen.*

'Conner?' Shivering violently and still restrained by the fishermen, Jayne looked at Flora blankly, as if she hadn't realised until this point who was trying to rescue her daughter. 'Conner MacNeil?'

'He's in the water now,' Flora said gently, wondering whether Jayne was going into shock. Her eyes were glazed and her face white. 'He's looking for her, Jayne.'

'Conner? When has he ever put his life on the line for anyone? He won't help her. *He won't help my baby.*' Her eyes suddenly wild with terror, Jayne developed superhuman strength, wrenched herself from the hold of the two men and hurled herself towards the edge of the quay once again.

The two men quickly grabbed her and she wriggled and pulled, struggling to free herself. 'Get the coastguard, any-one— Oh, God, no, no.' She collapsed, sobbing and Flora slid her arms round her, this time keeping her body between Jayne and the quay.

'Jayne, you're no help to Lily if you fall in, too. Leave it to Conner. You have to trust Conner.'

'Who in their right mind would trust Conner MacNeil?'

'I would,' Flora said simply, and realised that it was true. 'I'd trust him with my life.'

'Then you're obviously infatuated with him,' Jayne shrieked, 'like every other woman who comes close to him.' But she sagged against Flora, her energy depleted by the extravagant surge of emotion.

Infatuated?

Dismissing the accusation swiftly, Flora stared at the surface of the water but there was no movement and a couple of tourists standing next to her started to murmur dire predictions. She turned and glared at them just as there was a sound from the water and Conner surfaced, the limp, lifeless body of the child in his arms. He sucked in air and then hauled himself onto the concrete steps with one hand, his other arm holding the child protectively against his chest.

Lily lay still, her soaked dress darkened by blood, her hair streaked with it.

Flora felt panic, jagged and dangerous. Oh no, please no.

There were no signs of life. None.

Next to her Jayne started to moan like a creature tormented and then the sound stopped as she slid to the concrete in a faint.

'Leave her,' Conner ordered, climbing the steps out of the water, the body of the child still in his arms. Lily's head hung backwards and her skin was a dull grey colour. 'Someone else can look after her and at the moment she's better off out of it. Get me a towel, Flora. With the blood and the water, I can't see what we're dealing with here.'

A towel?

Feeling sick and shaky, Flora scanned the crowd and focused on two tourists who were loaded down with beach items. 'Give me your towel.' Without waiting for their permission, she yanked the towel out of the bag, spilling buckets and spades over the quay. Then she was on her knees beside Conner.

Lily lay pale and lifeless, her tiny body still, like a puppet that had been dropped. Blood spurted like a fountain from a wound on her leg.

'It's an artery.' With a soft curse Conner pressed down hard. 'I'm guessing she gashed it on the propeller as she fell. She's lucky the engine wasn't on.' He increased the pressure in an attempt to stop the bleeding. 'She's stopped breathing.'

Flora almost stopped breathing, too. Panic pressed in on her and without Connor's abrupt commands she would have shrivelled up and sobbed, just as Jayne had. Perhaps he realised that she was on the verge of falling apart because he lifted his head and glared at her, his blue eyes fierce with determination.

'Press here! I need to start CPR. Flora, *move*!'

She stared at him for a moment, so stunned by the enormity of what was happening she couldn't respond.

'Pull yourself together!' His tone was sharp. 'If we're to stand any chance here, I need some help, and you're the only person who knows what they're doing. Everyone else is just gawping.'

Flora felt suddenly dizzy. She'd never seen so much blood in her life. She'd never worked in A and E and all the first-aid courses she'd attended had been theoretical. *She didn't know what she was doing.*

And then she realised that *he* did. Conner knew exactly what he was doing and she knelt down beside him.

'Tell me what you want me to do.'

'Press here. Like that. That's it—good.' He put her hands on the wound, showed her just how hard he wanted her to press, and then shifted slightly so that he could focus on the child's breathing. With one hand on her forehead and the other under her chin, he gently tilted Lily's head back and covered her mouth with his, creating a seal. He breathed gently, watching as the child's chest rose.

Then he lifted his mouth and watched as Lily's chest fell as the air came out. 'Flora, get a tourniquet on that leg. She's losing blood by the bucketload.'

'A tourniquet?' Flora turned to the nearest tourist. 'Get me a bandage or a tie, something—anything—I can wind around her leg.'

The man simply stared at her, but his wife moved swiftly, jerking the tie from the neck of a businessman who had been waiting to take the ferry.

Flora didn't dare release the pressure on Lily's leg. 'If I let go to tie it, she's going to bleed.' Feeling horribly ignorant, she sent Conner a helpless glance. 'I haven't done this before. Do I put it directly over the wound?'

'Above the wound. You need a stick or something to twist it tight. Tie it and leave a gap and tie it again.'

Flora swiftly did as he instructed. The towel was soaked in blood and her fingers were slippery with it and shaking.

'The bleeding's not stopping Conner,' she muttered, and he glanced across at her, his expression hard.

'You need to tighten it. More pressure. Get a stick.'

She glanced at the uneven surface of the quay. 'There's no stick!'

'Then use something else!' He glared at the group of tourists standing nearest to them. 'Find a stick of some sort! A kid's spade, a cricket stump—anything we can use.'

'The blood is everywhere.' Flora tried to twist the tie tighter but the bleeding was relentless and she felt a sob build in her throat. It just seemed hopeless. Completely hopeless. 'She's four years old, Conner.' She was ready to give up but Conner placed the heel of his hand over the child's sternum.

'She's hypovolaemic. She needs fluid and she needs it fast.' He pushed down. 'Where the *hell* is the air ambulance?'

Someone thrust a stick into Flora's hand and she looked at it with relief. Perhaps now she could stop the bleeding. 'Do I push it under the tie and twist?'

'On top.' Conner stopped chest compressions and bent to give another rescue breath. 'Between the two knots. Twist. Make a note of the time—we can't leave it on for more than ten minutes. But if we're not out of here in ten minutes, it will be too late anyway.'

He covered Lily's mouth with his again and Flora followed his instructions, placing the stick between the first and second knots and twisting until it tightened.

'The air ambulance has just landed on the beach,' Jim, the ferryman, was by her shoulder, his voice surprisingly steady. 'What can I do, Flora?'

'I don't know. Keep the crowd away, I suppose. How's Jayne?'

'Out cold. Might be the best thing. Someone's looking after her—a nurse from the mainland on a day trip.'

Conner returned to chest compressions. 'Jim—get over to the paramedics. I want oxygen and plasma expander. And get them to radio the hospital and warn them. She's going to need whole blood or packed cells when she arrives. I want her in the air in the next few minutes. We don't have time to play around here.'

'Will do.' Without argument, Jim disappeared to do as Conner had instructed and Flora lifted the edge of the towel.

'The bleeding's stopped.' She felt weak with relief and Conner nodded.

'Good. We'll release it and check it in about ten minutes. If the bleeding doesn't start again we can leave it loose, but don't take it off—we might need it again.' He bent his head to give Lily another life-saving breath and Flora saw the paramedics sprinting along the quay towards them.

'They're here, Conner.'

Conner wasn't listening. His attention was focused on the child. 'Come on, baby girl,' he murmured softly, 'breathe for me.' His eyes were on her chest and Flora watched him, wondering. Had he seen something? Had he felt a change in her condition?

'Do you think she—?'

And at that moment Lily gave a choking cough and vomited weakly.

'Oh, thank God,' Flora breathed, and Conner turned the child's head gently and cleared her airway.

'There's a good girl. You're going to be all right now, sweetheart.'

He spoke so softly that Flora doubted that anyone else had heard his words of comfort and she felt a lump block her throat as she watched him with the child.

So he was capable of kindness, then. It was there, deep inside him, just as she'd always suspected.

But then he lifted his head and his eyes were hard as ever. 'Get some blankets, dry towels, coats—something to warm her up,' he ordered, and then looked at the paramedics. 'Give her some oxygen. I want to get a line in and give her a bolus of fluid and then we're out of here.'

'How much fluid do you want?'

Conner wiped his forearm across his brow, but he kept one hand on the child's arm. *Offering reassurance.* 'What's her weight? How old is she? We can estimate—'

'I know her weight exactly,' Flora said. 'I saw her in clinic last week. She's 16 kilograms. Do you want a calculator so that you can work out the fluid?'

'Start with 160 mils of colloid and then I'll reassess. I don't want to hang around here.' Conner released Lily's hand and started looking for a vein, while one of the paramedics sorted out the fluid and the other gave Lily some oxygen.

The child was breathing steadily now, her chest rising and falling as Conner worked. Occasionally her eyes fluttered open and then drifted closed again.

'She's got no veins,' Conner muttered, carefully examining Lily's arms. 'Get me an intraosseous needle. I'm not wasting time looking for non-existent veins. We need to get her to hospital. We've messed around here long enough.'

The paramedic dropped to his knees beside Conner, all the necessary equipment to hand. 'You want an intraosseous needle?'

'Actually, just give me a blue cannula. She might just have a vein I can use here.' Conner stroked the skin on the child's arm, focused. 'One go—if it fails, we'll get her in the air and I'll insert an intraosseous needle on the way.'

Flora leaned forward and closed her fingers around the child's arm, squeezing gently and murmuring words of reassurance. Lily was drifting in and out of consciousness and didn't seem aware of what was going on.

There was a commotion next to them but Conner didn't seem to notice. He didn't look up or hesitate. Instead, he applied himself to the task with total concentration, slid the needle into the vein and then gave a grunt of satisfaction. 'I'm in—good. That makes things easier. Let's flush it and tape it— I don't want to lose this line.'

The paramedic leaned towards him with tape but just at that moment Jayne launched herself at Conner and tried to drag him away. '*What are you doing to my baby?*' Her face was as white as swan's feathers, her eyes glazed with despair. 'Let me get to her— I need to hold her— *Get him away from her.*'

'Jayne, not now.' Flora quickly slid an arm round her shoulders and pulled her out of the way so that the paramedic and Conner could finish what they'd started.

'But she's dead,' Jayne moaned, and Flora shook her head.

'She's not dead, Jayne,' she said firmly. 'She's breathing.'

'Not dead?' Relief diluted the pain in Jayne's eyes but then panic rose again as she saw Conner bending over her child. '*What's he doing to her? Oh, God, there's blood everywhere.*'

'Lily cut herself very badly,' Flora began, but Jayne began to scream.

'Get him away from her! *Get him away from my baby! I don't trust him!*'

'You should trust him. He's the reason the bairn's breathing now.' It was Jim who spoke, his weatherbeaten face finally showing signs of strain. Gently but firmly he drew Jayne away from Flora. 'Flora, you help Dr MacNeil. Jayne, you're staying with me. And you'd better remember that Conner MacNeil is the reason Lily is alive right now. I know you're upset, and rightly so, but you need to get a hold. The man is working miracles.'

Conner straightened, conferred with the paramedics and together he and the crew transferred Lily's tiny form onto the stretcher. Then he wiped his blood-streaked hands down his soaked shorts. His handsome face was still damp with sea water and the expression in his ice-blue eyes cold and detached as he finally looked at Jayne. 'We're taking her to hospital.'

Jayne crumpled. 'I'm sorry, I'm so sorry.' Tears poured down her cheeks as she looked from him to Lily's still form. 'Can I come with you? Please?'

Conner took a towel that a tourist tentatively offered him. 'That depends on whether you're likely to assault me during the flight.' He wiped his hands properly, watching as Jayne breathed in and out and lifted a hand to her chest.

'I—I really am sorry.'

'No, you need to understand.' Conner handed the towel back, his voice brutally harsh. 'This isn't over. If she arrests during the flight, I'll be resuscitating her. Can you cope with that? Because if you can't, you're staying on the ground.'

Jayne flinched but for some reason his lack of sympathy seemed to help her pull herself together and find some dignity. 'I understand. Of course. And that's fine. I'm just grateful that you…' She swallowed and nodded. 'Do everything,' she whispered. 'Everything. I just—I just want to be near her. And with her when we get there. I— Thank you. Thank you so much.

Without you…' Her eyes met Conner's for a moment and he turned his attention back to Lily.

'We're wasting time. Let's move.'

In a matter of moments the helicopter was in the air and Flora watched as it swooped away from Glenmore towards the mainland.

Suddenly she realised how much her hands were shaking.

She stared down at herself. Her shorts were streaked with blood and Lily's blood still pooled on the grey concrete of the quay. 'Someone get a bucket and slosh some water over this,' she muttered to Jim, and he breathed a sigh and rubbed a hand over his face.

'I haven't seen anything like that in all my time on Glenmore.'

'No. I suppose it was because the quay was so crowded. She must have been knocked off the edge and into the water.'

'I didn't mean that.' Jim stared into the sky, watching as the helicopter shrank to a tiny dot in the distance. 'I meant Conner MacNeil. He was in the water like an arrow while the rest of us were still working out what had happened. And he just got on with it, didn't he?'

'Yes.' Flora cleared her throat. 'He did.'

'Logan says he was in the army.' Jim pushed his hat back from his forehead and scratched. 'I reckon if I was fighting in some godforsaken country, I'd feel better knowing he was around to pick up the pieces.'

'Yes. He was amazing.'

'He's not cuddly, of course.' Jim held up five fingers to a tourist who tentatively asked whether or not the ferry would be running. 'Five minutes. But in a crisis which do you prefer? Cuddly or competent?'

Flora swallowed, knowing that Jim was right. Conner's ice-cold assessment of the situation had been a huge part of the reason Lily was still alive. He hadn't allowed emotion to cloud his judgement, whereas she…

Suddenly Flora felt depression wash over her. The whole situation had been awful and she was experienced enough to know that, despite Conner's heroic efforts, Lily wasn't out of danger. 'I'd better go, Jim. I need to clean up.'

'And I need to get this ferry to the mainland.' Jim gave a wry smile and glanced at his watch. 'It's the first time the Glenmore ferry has been late since the service started. Nice job, Flora. Well done.'

But Flora knew that her part in the rescue had been minimal.

It had been Conner. All of it. He'd been the one to dive into the water. He'd pulled Lily out. And when she'd been frozen with panic at the sight of Lily's lifeless form covered in all that blood, he'd worked with ruthless efficiency, showing no emotion but getting the job done. Nothing had distracted him. Not even Lily's mother. He'd had a task to do and he'd done it.

CHAPTER SIX

SHE COULDN'T relax at home so she went back to the beach with her book and when it was too dark to read she just sat, listening to the hiss of the waves as they rushed forward onto the beach and then retreated.

She wanted to know how Lily was faring, but Conner wasn't answering his mobile and she didn't want to bother the hospital staff.

Shrieks of excitement came from the far corner of the beach where a group of teenagers had lit a fire and were having a beach party. Flora watched for a moment, knowing that she was too far away for them to see her. They weren't supposed to light fires but they always did. This was Glenmore in the summer. She knew that sooner or later Nick Hillier, the policeman, would do one of his evening patrols and if they were still there, he'd move them on. Back home to their parents or the properties they rented for a few weeks every summer.

'What's a nice girl like you doing on a beach like this? It's late. You should be home.' The harsh, familiar male voice came from directly behind her and she gave a gasp of shock.

'Conner? Where did you come from? I thought you'd still be on the mainland.'

'Hitched a lift back on a boat.'

'How's Lily?'

'Asking for her dolls.'

Flora felt a rush of relief and smiled. 'That's wonderful.'

'If it's wonderful, why such a long face?' He sat down next to her and there was enough light for her to see the dark stains on his shirt and trousers. It was a vivid reminder of just what he'd achieved.

'It would have been a very different outcome for Lily if you hadn't been there.'

'Someone else would have done it.'

'No. No, they wouldn't. And I was no use to you at all. I'm sorry. I was completely out of my depth. I've never seen anything like that before.' Just the thought of Lily's body, lifeless and covered with blood, made her feel sick.

'You were fine.' He reached behind him for a pebble and threw it carelessly into the darkness. There was a faint splash as it hit the water.

'Conner, I wasn't fine.' She'd been thinking about it all evening and becoming more and more upset. 'You always imagine that you'll know what to do in an emergency, but I didn't. I didn't know! I mean, I suppose I knew the theory but nothing prepares you for seeing a little girl you know well, covered in blood and not breathing. I—I just couldn't concentrate.'

'That happens to the best of us.'

She was willing to bet it had never happened to him. 'I've never even tied a tourniquet before.'

'Join the army,' he suggested, and reached for another stone. 'You get to tie quite a few. Believe me, it's a talent I'd willingly not have to use ever again. You were fine. Stop worrying.'

'There was so much blood.'

'Yeah—it has a habit of spreading itself around when you hit an artery.'

'It didn't worry you.'

'Blood?' He shrugged. 'No, blood doesn't worry me—but emotion…' He gave a hollow laugh and threw the stone. 'Now that's a different story. When they discharge her from hospital, you're the one that's visiting.'

She curled her toes into the soft sand. 'I remember Jayne from school.'

'Me, too. I think I might have kissed her once.'

'You kissed everyone.' *Except her.* She turned to look at him. Fresh stubble darkened his jaw and in the dim light he looked more dangerous than ever.

He flung another stone and then leaned back on his elbows, watching her through narrowed eyes. 'What the hell are you doing out here at this hour, Flora Harris? You should be tucked up in bed, having exhausted yourself with a fat book.'

Flora drew a circle in the sand with her finger. 'You think I'm so boring, don't you?'

'Trust me, you don't want to know what I think.'

'I already know.' Her heart thumping, she looked at him. 'I'm probably the only girl on Glenmore that you haven't kissed, so that says quite a lot.'

'It says that I still had some decency, despite what the locals thought of me. You weren't exactly the kind of girl to indulge in adolescent groping.' Conner glanced towards the crowd on the beach, barely visible in the darkness. 'You didn't do late-night beach orgies. I suppose you were studying.'

'Yes, I probably was.' Flora thought of the life she'd led. 'Dad hated me being out too late. He always worried about me.'

'You were a good daughter. You never once slipped off the rails, not even for a moment. That's good. Be proud of it.'

'It was easy to stay on the rails because my rails were smooth and consistent. I lost Mum but I still had Dad.' She glanced at him, hesitant about saying something that would upset him. 'It must be very stressful for you, coming back here after so long. You had such a difficult childhood and all the memories are here.'

'Actually, I think I probably had an easier childhood than

you. Everyone expected you to do well, so you had to work hard and deliver or risk disappointing them. No one expected anything but trouble when I was around, so I could create havoc and meet their expectations at the same time.' He sat up and flung another stone. 'Your father expected you to be home before dark because he loved you and worried about you, so you didn't dare go out and paint the town red in case you upset him. My father didn't give a damn what I did as long as it didn't involve him.'

'You must be very upset and angry with your mother for leaving.'

'Not at all.' His tone was cool. 'He beat her every day of their marriage. She had no choice but to get out. She should have done it sooner. Probably would have done if it hadn't been for me.'

Flora was so shocked by his unexpected confession that it took her a moment to respond. 'Oh, Conner...' She'd heard rumours, of course, but no one had ever known for sure. 'But she left you there. With him.'

'She had no choice about that. If she'd taken me, he would have followed. Her only chance was to go before he killed her.'

Flora sat for a moment, trying to imagine what it must have been like, and failing. She'd only ever known love. 'Did he ever...?' Her voice trailed off and she shook her head and looked away. 'Sorry, it's none of my business and I know you hate talking about personal stuff.'

'Did he ever hit me? Is that what you were about to ask?' He lay back on the sand and stared into the darkness. 'Just once. And I was so angry I stabbed a hole in his leg with a kitchen knife. I was six years old at the time. After that he left me alone. I think he was always a bit worried I'd empty the contents of the science lab into his tea. Did you know that science was the only subject I never skipped? I went through a phase of making bombs—blowing everything up. You probably remember that phase. Everyone on Glenmore does.'

Flora hesitated and then reached out and touched his arm, because it seemed like the right thing to do. 'I can't imagine what it must have been like for you.'

'It was amazing fun. I was causing explosions all over the place and no one could stop me.' He showed no emotion but she wasn't fooled.

'So if it's that easy and you care so little, why haven't you come home before now?'

'Good question.' He was silent for a moment and then he laughed. 'Perceptive, aren't you? Yes, I suppose I'm back here because I wanted to see how it felt to be home.'

'And?'

'It feels every bit as bad as I thought it would.' He spoke calmly and turned his head to look at her. 'So now I've spilled my guts, what happens next? I cry into your soft bosom and get in touch with my feelings?'

'In case you hadn't noticed, I'm pretty flat-chested so that won't work.' She kept her tone light because she sensed that was what he wanted. 'I suppose I just want you to know that, well, that I'm a friend—if you need one.'

'A flat-chested friend.' He gave a slow smile. 'I've never had one of those before. Do you know what I really fancy right now?'

Her heart thumped wildly. 'I hardly dare ask.'

'A cigarette.'

It wasn't what she'd wanted him to say and she let out a breath, not knowing whether to laugh or cry. *Drop the fantasies*, Flora. 'I didn't know you smoked.'

'I don't. At least, not for years. I just need something to relieve the tension. I'll have to find another way.'

Flora stiffened. *He was talking about sex*, she knew he was. And there was no doubt in her mind that there were any number of women on Glenmore who would be only too delighted to offer him the distraction he wanted.

And he was stuck on the beach with her.

Boring Flora.

He looked at her. 'I suppose it's a waste of time asking if you have any cigarettes?'

'Complete waste of time,' she said lightly. *Boring, staid Flora.*

'Anything to drink?'

'I have a small bottle of mineral water in my bag.'

'Mineral water?' He laughed. 'You really know how to live, don't you? Nothing like a few minerals to get a person into a party mood. Tell me, Flora Harris, what do you do to release tension? Read a chapter of *War and Peace*?'

She smiled. 'If I can't sail, then I swim.'

'You swim?'

'In the sea. Every morning. I love it. It relaxes me.'

'You take your clothes off?'

'No, I swim in my uniform.' Flora glanced at him in amusement. 'Of course I take my clothes off. What did you think?'

'I've no idea. I've made a point of never picturing you without clothes on.'

'Thanks.'

His eyes narrowed. 'If you're taking that as an insult then you're even more naïve than I think you are.'

'I'm not naïve.'

'Yes, you are. The reason I don't picture you without clothes is because then I'll start thinking about you in a way that would make Logan punch me.'

Her heart was racing. 'Logan isn't my keeper.'

'Good point.' He rose to his feet and tugged her up beside him. 'Come on, then, Flora Harris. We'll try the swim. See if it works.'

'Now?' Her voice was an astonished squeak. 'It's one in the morning.'

'Less crowded than one in the afternoon.'

She gave a strangled laugh. 'Yes, I suppose it is. I don't have a costume.'

He gave a wicked smile and slowly undid the buttons on his shirt. 'The point of skinny dipping is that you don't need clothes.' His hands dropped to the fastening at the waistband of his trousers and her cheeks warmed as she caught a glimpse of taut, muscular stomach and dark male body hair.

'For goodness' sake, Conner…'

'What? You just said "Of course I take my clothes off." So that's what I'm doing.'

'Obviously, I wear a costume.'

'Obviously.' He grinned. 'Because you wouldn't be you if you didn't. But me being me, I'm not going to bother.' Completely unselfconscious, he stepped out of his trousers and boxer shorts and Flora gave a nervous laugh, keeping her eyes firmly fixed on the horizon.

'You're going to get yourself arrested, Conner MacNeil.'

'It's dark. No one knows we're here.' His hands were on the hem of her T-shirt. 'Come on, Flora. Take a risk. Live a little. Get naked with me.'

Take a risk. Live a little.

Suddenly the world opened up in front of her and her heart thundered in her chest. 'I am *not* swimming naked with you.'

'If the water is as cold as I suspect it's going to be, you're at no risk from me, darling, but if it makes you feel better you can leave your underwear on.' He gently pulled the T-shirt over her head and slid her shorts down her legs.

As his fingers brushed her skin and she shivered.

She knew she should stop him, but she couldn't, and when he closed his hand firmly over hers and dragged her down to the water's edge, she didn't resist.

And then the water touched her feet and she stopped dead. 'Oh, my goodness, that's cold.'

'Don't be a wimp.' He jerked her forward. 'This was your idea and you're not bottling out now. Anyway, what are you complaining about?' Conner kept walking, long steady strides that took him deeper into the sea. 'It's like bathwater. I can't imagine why anyone would travel all the way to the Mediterranean when we have this on our doorstep.' He gave her no choice but to wade in with him and she picked her way gingerly through the dark, swirling water, catching her breath as the waves licked higher and higher on her legs.

'I'm not sure if I like doing this in the middle of the night.' She peered towards her feet. 'Do you think there are jellyfish?'

'No. It's long past their bedtime. They're all curled up asleep with hot-water bottles.' The water was halfway up his thighs now and as a wave washed over him at waist level, he cursed fluently. 'I think we've just discovered a whole new non-surgical method of vasectomy. If any of my sperm survive this experience, it will be a miracle.'

Flora giggled helplessly and wondered what had come over her. *What was she doing?* She was standing in the sea at one o'clock in the morning with Conner MacNeil, the most dangerous, unsuitable man she was every likely to meet.

And she was having the time of her life.

'This is freezing. I don't think I can go in any further.'

'The only way to do this is quickly. If you do this every morning then I have new respect for you, Flora. You're twice the woman I thought you were, flat chest or no flat chest.'

'It's bracing. It wakes me up.'

'No surprise there. If this didn't wake you up, you'd have to be dead.'

'It's colder tonight.' She clutched him tightly, afraid that the waves would knock her over, and he steadied her and then released her hand.

'All right, let's do this…' He dived forward into the waves and she had a brief glimpse of powerful male muscle and strong legs before he vanished from sight.

She rubbed her hands down her arms, knowing that the goose-bumps had nothing to do with the cold water and everything to do with the way her body had felt next to his. *How*

*was it possible to feel hot when she was standing waist deep
in freezing seawater?*

She followed him into the waves, wondering why she'd
never swum in the moonlight before. In all the years she'd lived
here and swum here, she'd never done this. And it was
fabulous. Magical. The stars and the moon shone in the clear
sky and the water glistened.

And she felt daring and more alive than she'd ever felt.

She was so enchanted by her surroundings that she gasped
with shock when Conner emerged next to her.

There was just enough light for her to see the outline of his
face and the faint glitter in his eyes as he reached out and
pulled her against him. 'I can't believe I'm skinny dipping with
Flora Harris. Looks like I've finally corrupted you.'

'I like being corrupted.' She kept her voice light, trying not
to reveal how it felt to be this close to him. She could feel the
hardness of his thighs against hers and, despite his complaints
about the cold water, a building pressure against her abdomen.
'And I'm not naked.'

'Not yet.'

'Conner...' To keep her balance she placed her hands on his
shoulders and felt the smooth swell of hard male muscle under
her fingers.

His mouth was dangerously close to hers. 'I've been
thinking about what you said.'

Thinking? *How could he think?* 'What did I say?'

'That you were the only female on the island that I haven't
kissed.'

'I was wrong.' She was so aware of him that could barely
speak, 'I'm fairly sure you haven't kissed Ann Carne, and Mrs
Parker may have escaped, too.'

'Good point.' He lifted his hands and cupped her face gently.
'Nevertheless, it's only fair to warn you that I might be about
to corrupt you further. You might want to run for the beach. I'll
give you a two-second start.'

Her heart pounded like the hooves of a racehorse on the home stretch. 'Two seconds doesn't sound like much.'

'It's all you're getting. Take it or leave it.'

She couldn't take her eyes from his and the anticipation was agonising. 'I'll leave it. I can't run in these waves.' *He was going to kiss her.*

Finally, after what seemed like a lifetime, Conner MacNeil was going to kiss her.

'If you can't run, then you're trapped.' His head moved closer but he didn't touch her. Instead, his mouth hovered tantalisingly close to hers, the expression in his eyes knowing and wickedly sexy as he prolonged the torture for both of them. Her stomach tumbled and her senses hummed and when finally he brushed his lips over hers, she knew that this was the most perfect and exciting thing that had ever happened to her. His lips were cool and the tip of his tongue gently caressed her lower lip.

Heat exploded inside her and she made a soft sound in her throat and leaned against him, seeking more. Her eyes closed, but still she saw stars as everything inside her erupted with excitement.

His fingers closed hard around her arms and his body shifted against hers.

'Hell, Flora...' This time his mouth came down hard, his kiss sending bolts of electricity through her body, and she clutched at him for support as he drew the fire from deep inside her with the skilled, sensual stroke of his tongue. And she kissed him back, her tongue toying with his in a kiss that was both intimate and erotic. His hands dropped from her face and slid down her back, pulling her against him in a movement that was unmistakably possessive.

It was a kiss with promise and purpose but before she had the chance to discover where it was leading, there was a shout.

With a groan of frustration and anger Conner dragged his mouth from hers and Flora clutched at him for support, dizzy and disoriented from the kiss. It took her a moment to realise that the sound was coming from the beach behind them.

'Conner? Conner MacNeil, is that you? It's Jim—Jim from the ferry and a few of the lads. We wanted to buy you a drink.'

'Oh, my goodness.' Flora shrank with embarrassment. 'They can't possibly see us, can they? It's too dark.'

Conner stared down at her for a moment, his lashes lowered, his eyes as cool and defiant as ever. 'Do you care?'

Flora didn't answer because she genuinely didn't know the answer to that. This was her island. And it was her reputation on the line. She should care, she knew she should. But his kiss had changed everything. It was as if her life had reached a crossroads and she didn't know which path to take—the safe one was back on the shore and the dangerous one was here, in the sea, with Conner's hard male body pressed against hers.

'Flora?' His voice was even and she wondered how he could sound so normal after what they'd shared. She felt far from normal. She felt churned up, confused—*different*.

She breathed in and out. She knew that it was too dark for them to have recognised her, but if she walked out of the water with Conner…

She wanted to say, *Damn the lot of them,* and carry on kissing him, but something held her back. 'I—I don't know, Conner.' Her fingers tightened on his arms. 'I suppose I do care. I have to work with these people. I'll still be living on this island long after you've left.'

He released her abruptly. 'Of course you will. Stay here. I'll get them away from you and you can get home before anyone is any the wiser. I guess that's more chivalrous than escorting you home.' He spoke with a careless indifference and she felt a flash of desperation as she sensed his withdrawal and felt her new self slipping away.

Suddenly she wished desperately that she hadn't spoken. *The person who had spoken had been the girl she'd been all her life, but now she wasn't sure if she was that girl any more. She didn't know if she wanted to be that girl.*

She wanted to be daring and careless of the consequences, like him. She wanted to live in the moment and not think about what other people thought. She wanted to kiss Conner MacNeil and enjoy every second of the excitement.

Without his hands to steady her, she almost stumbled as a wave hit her from the back and the shower of cold water seemed symbolic.

It was over.

Her moment of wild living had passed and she was back to being boring Flora. Sensible Flora. A girl who would never swim half-naked in the sea with a very unsuitable man.

But did she really want to be that girl?

'Conner, wait.' She grabbed his arm. 'I don't care about them. I don't care if they see us.'

It took him a moment to reply and when he did, his voice was rough. 'Yes, you do, angel. And quite right, too. How are you going to have a proper conversation with Mrs Parker if word gets round that you've been cavorting in the waves with Bad Conner? Be grateful to the locals. You've been saved from total corruption by the brave and persistent citizens of Glenmore.'

She didn't know what to say to rescue the situation so she tried to joke about it. 'Isn't it typical? The first time I try to be wild, I have an audience.'

He laughed, then lifted a hand and drew his thumb slowly over her lower lip, the intimacy of the gesture in direct contrast to his words. 'I've had more excitement being shot at in the desert.' His tone was sarcastic but the look in his eyes made her dizzy.

'I'm sure.'

His smile faded. 'You're not made for this, Flora, and both of us know it. You need a man you're not ashamed to be seen with, so let's end this now before we both do something that will keep the locals talking for years. I'll swim to the other side of the beach and meet them there. Stay in the water until I'm out and they won't see you. Can you make your way home safely?'

'Of course. Do I look helpless?'

'No, you look sexy.' He gave a wicked smile and lowered his mouth to hers once more, his lips and tongue working a seductive magic that made the world spin. Then he lifted his head reluctantly and gave a resigned shrug. 'Sorry about that. Just couldn't help myself. Once bad, always bad, or so it would seem. You just had a lucky escape, Flora Harris. Five more minutes and we would have been in the middle of a practical scientific experiment involving frozen body parts and libido.' Without giving her time to respond, he called to the men on the shore. 'Back off, guys. I'll be with you in a minute.' And then he plunged back into the waves and swam away from her with a powerful crawl.

Nodding to the locals who were toasting his health, Conner raised his glass to his lips and tried to decide whether he should be grateful or just punch them.

Five minutes more and he would have been completing the corruption of Flora.

So he should be grateful, obviously. If he'd followed the episode to its natural conclusion, Flora would now be steeped in embarrassment and regret.

He remembered her anguished gasp when she'd realised that they'd been spotted. Even in the semi-darkness he'd been able to see the burning colour of her cheeks.

Narrow escape for her. And for him, he told himself firmly. It was hard enough being back on Glenmore, without having that on his conscience.

He drank deeply, trying to obliterate the memory of the way she'd tasted and the way her body had felt pressed against his. She'd been lithe, slender, slippery from the seawater—

'Conner MacNeil, am I drunk or are you really sitting there drinking cranberry juice?'

Conner looked at Jim. 'You are drunk. And I am sitting here drinking cranberry juice.'

Jim focused on the glass in his hand. 'It looks disgusting.'

'It is disgusting.' *But not as disgusting as Evanna's home-made lemonade*, he thought with wry humour. Something stirred inside him as he remembered Flora standing on the grass, clutching a picnic basket.

'When I offered to buy you a drink…' Jim lifted a finger and waggled it in his direction '…I meant a *proper* drink. A man's drink. What are you? Wimp or man?'

Dismissing thoughts of Flora's soft mouth, Conner gave a careless lift of his shoulder. 'Wimp, obviously.'

'Leave the man alone.' Nick Hillier, the island policeman, slapped Conner on the back. 'A hero can relax in any way he chooses. Personally, I'm just glad it's not alcohol. It will save me the bother of arresting him for drink-driving later.'

Jim hiccoughed lightly. 'Your old man knew how to drink.'

An uncomfortable silence fell on the group of men who'd had less to drink than Jim, but Conner simply nodded. 'He certainly did.'

Jim sniffed. 'Couldn't have been easy, living with that. Duncan MacNeil had one hell of a temper.'

'You want me to cry on your shoulder?'

Jim shuddered. 'You know what I want? I want to know who the girl was, Conner. That's what I want.' He winked at the others and Conner slowly lowered his glass to the table.

So they *had* seen. 'No one.'

'Bet she was pretty. You always did get the pretty ones. Hey, everyone…,' Jim raised his voice to attract maximum attention. Then he hiccoughed again and lifted his glass in salute. 'Conner was in the waves with "no one".'

'At least "no one" can't nag at you,' someone muttered, and Jim gave a snort.

'She was real enough.'

'We can torture it out of him.' Nick suggested. 'You have the right to remain silent—'

'And I intend to,' Conner drawled, his face expressionless. Inside, a slow anger burned. *Anger towards himself and what he'd so nearly done.* If they'd seen that it was Flora, what would that have done to her reputation? She was decent and sweet and, as she'd pointed out, she was going to be working on this island long after he'd turned his back on it for ever. She was also a shy and private person who would have hidden in a hole in the ground rather than have her name tossed carelessly around a group of men in a pub.

And with his selfish actions, he'd almost destroyed everything she'd worked for.

And not just by exposing her to gossip.

He lifted his glass again, remembering the shyness and the desperate excitement in her eyes in the last seconds before he'd given in to impulse and kissed her. She'd wanted him, badly. He should have been flattered but instead he felt…disgusted with himself. Disgusted with himself for not walking away. He had no idea how much sexual experience she'd had, but he was willing to bet that her lifestyle didn't encompass meaningless affairs, and that was all he could offer her.

He stared at the bunch of locals gathered around the table, laughing and joking at his expense.

He should be grateful to them.

If it weren't for them he'd now be suffering from regret instead of sexual frustration. And Flora… Flora would have assured him in that polite voice of hers that everything was fine, but deep down she'd have been horrified at herself for indulging in a moment of madness with a delinquent like him.

Or worse—she'd be looking at him with those huge, brown eyes of hers, wanting things from him that he'd never, ever be able to deliver.

Conner drained his glass, knowing that probably for the first time in his life he'd done the right thing.

With a humourless laugh he studied the empty glass in his hand, sure of one thing. If doing the right thing felt this bad, he wasn't going to make a habit of it.

CHAPTER SEVEN

'HE SAVED the child, can you believe that? Anyway, I always knew there was good in him. It's not surprising he went off the rails with everything that he had to contend with at home.' Angela Parker watched as Flora tightened the bandage. 'I mean, his mother left when he was only ten years old. And his father was a drunk. A *violent* drunk, some say. Shocking, really shocking. It's no wonder he was wild. The poor boy.'

'Yes, Mrs Parker. I mean, no.' Flora was barely listening. Her mind was on other things. Although part of her was delighted and relieved that the entire island was now treating Conner as a hero, another part of her felt as though something inside her had been ripped out.

It was just because she was tired, she told herself. But she knew that wasn't true. It had nothing to do with lack of sleep and everything to do with the kiss she'd shared with Conner.

The kiss that had been interrupted.

The kiss that she'd totally messed up.

She kept reliving that moment and wishing she'd done things differently. She wished she'd yelled out, *It's me, Flora Harris, Jim. Yes, I'm kissing Conner so could you just all go away and let us get on with it?* She wished she hadn't been embarrassed. She wished she'd held onto the moment instead of letting it slip from her fingers. She wished…

She wished Conner felt something for her.

But he didn't.

In fact, not only had he not mentioned it, he hadn't even talked to her. Several days had passed and he'd been so busy fielding patients eager to consult him about his various problems that she'd barely seen him in the distance, let alone put herself in the position where a conversation might be possible.

At first she'd managed to convince herself that he was just very busy. She'd lingered in the surgery long after the patients had left, hoping that he'd seek her out, and she'd sat in her empty cottage at night, waiting for a knock on the door or the ring of the phone.

She'd thought up a million reasons for the fact that he hadn't come near her, but in the end she'd run out of reasons. And still he hadn't disturbed her solitude.

And she couldn't blame him for that, could she? Not after she'd made it perfectly clear that she'd be embarrassed to be caught with him. It was hardly surprising that he was now avoiding her and she wished she'd done everything differently.

She had no backbone.

She was pathetic.

'Well?' Angela peered down at her. 'You've been staring at my leg for ages, dear. Is something wrong?'

'No, nothing,' Flora said quickly, and Angela nodded.

'If you're worried, perhaps I should make an appointment with Conner.'

Remembering how fast Angela had run from Conner just a couple of weeks ago, Flora gave a faint smile. That was the other reason she was finding it hard to put him out of her head. Everywhere she went, people were talking about Conner. And he treated their attention with as much careless indifference as he'd treated their disregard.

'Your leg is looking much better, Mrs Parker. The inflammation has settled and I think it's healing now. Keep up the good work.'

And she had to pull herself together and accept the person she was. She just wasn't someone who could cavort half-naked in the moonlight with the island bad boy. She cared too much what people thought.

And that was why a relationship between her and Conner would never work.

She cared. And Conner didn't give a damn. The more he shocked people, the happier he was.

Even that night on the beach had probably just been a game to him, seeing if his seduction skills were good enough to persuade boring old Flora to kiss him.

He wasn't interested in anything more, and she couldn't blame him for that.

She was boring Flora, wasn't she? The type of girl who kept her knickers on even when she swam in the sea at night.

Not the sort of girl who would hold Conner MacNeil's attention for more than two minutes.

Trying to block out Angela's endless chatter, Flora finished the dressing, washed her hands, completed her notes and saw the woman to the door.

Then she went across and tapped on Logan's door. 'How's Evanna?'

'Still pregnant. No change. She's going to the mainland for a check at the end of the week.'

'And presumably you can go with her now, given that the entire population of Glenmore thinks that Conner walks on water.'

'I know. It's brilliant. Overnight my life has changed.' He smiled at her. 'I actually managed to have breakfast with my wife and daughter this morning. Conner should be a hero more often. I could resign and grow my own vegetables.'

'I'm so pleased it's all worked out. His surgery is so full now Janet's having to turn people away.'

'Conner's a good doctor.'

'Yes.' She thought of him with Lily. *His sure touch. His skill.*

His incredible focus when the entire world around him had been panicking.

And then she thought of his kiss. Equally sure and skilled. Did he do everything well?

She gave a little shiver and Logan glanced at her.

'Are you all right? You're a bit pale.'

'I'm fine. Absolutely fine.' Just confused. *Frustrated. Out of her depth.* She'd never felt like this before and she didn't know what to do about it. Her previous relationships had been boringly uncomplicated. She'd been out with two men and neither of them had caused this degree of turbulence to her insides. 'Tell Evanna to call me if she needs anything.'

'I'll do that.' Logan studied her closely. 'Are you sure you're all right?'

'Really, I'm fine,' Flora lied. 'Just a little tired.'

'Right.' Logan watched her. 'If you're sure.'

Flora returned to her consulting room and worked her way through her patients, only half listening to the steady stream of Glenmore chatter.

She'd just seen her last patient when the door opened and Conner stood there.

Flora felt her stomach flip and looked at his face, hoping to see something that suggested he felt the same way, but there was nothing. His handsome face was expressionless, his attitude brisk and professional.

'Lily is being discharged today. You should call on her and her fussy mother—do all the touchy-feely stuff that I can't be bothered with.'

She tried not to feel hurt or disappointed. *What had she expected?* 'You could go yourself. They'd want to thank you. Jayne is so grateful, she can't stop crying.'

'All the more reason to stay away. The one body fluid I'm no good with is female tears.' He gave a faint smile. 'If Lily bleeds again, phone me. Otherwise it's just emotional support and someone else can do that bit. Someone better qualified than me.'

He wasn't comfortable with emotion.

Flora thought of the things he'd told her in the velvet darkness. She thought about the mother who had left him and the father who hadn't cared. And she suspected that he'd been exposed to more extremes of emotion in his childhood than most people experienced in a lifetime.

Was that why he backed away from it now?

Was that why he was backing away from *her*?

'I'll call on her.'

'Good.' His eyes held hers for a moment—lingered—then his mouth tightened and he turned to leave.

But there had been something in that look that made it impossible for her to let him walk away. 'Conner!' Something burst free inside her and she just couldn't help herself. 'Wait. Can we talk?'

Conner paused, his hand on the door, a man poised for flight. 'What about?' But he knew what it was going to be about and he kept his tone cool and his face expressionless because he also knew what he needed to do. *And it was going to be the hardest thing he'd ever done.*

He stood still, hoping she'd lose courage. And perhaps she almost did because she watched him closely and then gave a confused little smile that cut through him like the blade of a knife.

Don't say it, Flora. Don't say it and then I won't have to reject you.

She rubbed her hands nervously down her uniform and took a deep breath. 'All I wanted to say was that…well, you—you really don't have to avoid me.'

'Yes, I do.' He kept his answer blunt, knowing that it was the only way.

'Why? Because you kissed me?' She shrugged awkwardly. 'Do you ignore every woman you kiss?'

'No, normally I corrupt them totally before I ignore them. You escaped lightly.'

'Is that supposed to make me feel lucky?' The colour bloomed in her cheeks but she didn't back off. 'Because it doesn't.'

Her response almost weakened him and Conner reminded himself ruthlessly that this time he was doing the right thing, not the easy thing.

He watched her for a moment, his eyes fixed on her face. Then he closed the door, slowly and deliberately, giving them privacy. 'It should make you feel lucky. If they hadn't turned up I would have taken you, Flora.' His voice dangerously soft, he closed the distance between them in a single stride. *Shock tactics.* Perhaps shock tactics would work. 'You would have been mine. That's how close you came.'

She shivered with excitement. 'Yes…'

'And then I would have dumped you, because that's what I do with women. And you would have cried.'

She swallowed. 'Maybe.'

Definitely.

Unable to help himself, Conner lifted a hand to touch her but then saw the trust shining in her dark eyes and took a step backwards, letting his hand drop to his side. 'You're the sort of woman who deserves to wake up next to a good man.' His hand curled into a fist. 'That isn't me, Flora.'

'You're a good man.'

'No.'

'Why do you say that?'

'Because a good man wouldn't do what I'm about to do,' he muttered, knowing that he'd lost the fight. He reached out a hand, yanking her against him and crushing his mouth against hers.

A kaleidoscope of colours exploded in his head and any

hope of pulling away vanished as she wrapped her arms around his neck and pressed closer. He kissed her roughly but she gave back willingly and her mouth was sweet and warm under his.

And since when had sweetness had any place in his life?

He released her so suddenly that she swayed dizzily. 'Conner—'

'Don't.' With a rough jerk he disengaged himself from her arms. 'Don't offer yourself to me, Flora.'

'Why not?' Clearly sensing the tension and anger boiling inside him, she lifted a hand to his cheek, pushing aside her natural shyness. 'It's what I want.'

'No, it isn't what you want.'

She stood, looking hurt and vulnerable. 'It is. I want you.'

The blood throbbing in his veins, Conner turned away from her, knowing that he couldn't say what he had to say if he was looking at her. None of the things he'd ever done in his life had ever felt as hard as this and he steeled himself to do what had to be done. 'Well, I don't want you.' His tone was rock steady. 'I'm sorry if that hurts, but it's better to be honest up front. I don't want you, Flora. There's no chemistry there at all.'

Her soft gasp was like a punch in the gut. 'Conner—'

'You kiss like a child, Flora. You don't even turn me on.' This time he altered his tone so that he sounded careless, even a little bored. Then he gave a dismissive shrug and strolled towards the door. 'I suggest you find someone of your own age to practise on.'

Then he left the room, slamming the door so hard that the entire building shook.

Only when he was safely within the privacy of his consulting room did Conner finally release the emotion he'd kept firmly locked inside. He let out a string of expletives and thumped his fist against the wall. Then he sank onto his chair and stared at the door, willing himself not to walk back through it and tell her that he hadn't meant a single word he'd just said.

Because if he did that—*if he sought her out and apologised*—he wouldn't be righting a wrong, he'd be making things worse.

Yes, he'd hurt her.

He'd hurt her so badly that he felt physically sick at the thought, and he knew that her gasp of pain and the shimmer of tears in her eyes would stay with him for a long time.

But he also knew that the pain would be infinitely greater if he took their relationship any further.

His eyes slid to the doorhandle and he gritted his teeth and looked away, ruthlessly ignoring the urge to go back and comfort her. Talk to her. What was there to say? He'd already said it. And better now than later. Better a small amount of private pain than public humiliation when the entire island discovered their affair.

They'd tear her apart and he wasn't going to let that happen to her.

There was a tap on the door and he looked up with a growl of impatience, furious at having been disturbed. 'What?' He barked the word and the door opened slowly and a woman peeped nervously into the room.

'Janet said to come straight through.'

'What for?'

She blinked. 'Surgery? I have an appointment with you.'

Conner stared at her blankly and then realised that kissing Flora had actually driven everything out of his head. *Everything, including the fact that he was supposed to be seeing patients.*

'Of course. Sorry.' He managed something approximating a smile. 'Come in.' And then he recognised her. Agatha Patterson, the elderly lady who lived in the converted lifeboat cottage on the beach. 'I expect you've come to exact your revenge. I seem to remember raiding your flower-beds one night.'

'You gave them to that girl—the pretty blonde one. I still remember how pleased she was.'

Conner gave a faint smile. 'That was at least sixteen years ago so I'm guessing you're not here because you're worried about your memory. Am I supposed to apologise for helping myself to your flowers?'

'Goodness, I don't want an apology! I should be the one thanking you.' Agatha closed the door and walked stiffly into the room. 'You livened up my life. You were always down on the beach below my property. I liked watching you.'

Remembering some of the things he'd done on the beach below her house, Conner inhaled sharply. 'How much could you see?'

'Well, my eyes were better in those days, of course.' She chuckled and walked slowly towards the chair, her body bent in the shape of a question mark. She was a grey-haired lady with a jolly smile and a twinkle in her eye that hinted at a lively past. 'I was always amazed by how successful you were. Quite the lad, Conner MacNeil.'

Conner gave a reluctant laugh. 'All right, that's probably enough of that conversation. Did you want to ask me something or are you just here to threaten me with my wicked past?'

'Oh, no, nothing like that. I heard what you did for little Lily, by the way. I think you're amazing.'

'Thanks.' *So amazing that he'd left a woman crying in the room opposite.* 'What can I do for you, Mrs Patterson?'

'Well, funnily enough, it's my eyes I've come about. They're incredibly sore.'

'Too much watching people on the beach,' Conner said in a wry tone, and she gave a delighted smile.

'There's been hardly any action since you left. These days everyone is too worried about being arrested. Not that you ever worried about that sort of thing. Anyway, I wouldn't normally bother you with anything so pathetically trivial, but my eyes are so sore that the pain is reducing the time I can spend on the internet.'

Conner stared at her. 'The *internet*?'

'And if you're thinking of telling me to reduce the time I spend on the computer, you needn't waste your breath. I'm careful never to do more than eight hours a day.'

Conner glanced at his own computer screen, searching for the information he wanted. 'You're...eighty-six, Mrs Patterson. Is that right?'

'Eighty-seven next week.'

'And you're spending...' he cleared his throat, intrigued by his patient '...*how long* on the internet?'

'No more than eight hours a day.' She curled her fingers around the strap of her bag. 'Given the chance, I'd spent longer, but with my eyes the way they are...'

Conner gave a disbelieving laugh. 'I have to ask this—just what are you doing on the internet, Mrs Patterson?'

'Everything,' she said simply. 'I mean, for an old lady on her own like me, it's a doorway to a whole new exciting life. Last week I spent a morning looking around a new exhibition in a fancy gallery in London, just by clicking my mouse, then I spent an afternoon gazing at a beach in Australia—amazing webcam, by the way, you should try it. Last month I spent an entire week in Florence—I visited somewhere new every day. But it's not just travel and art, it's food, conversation. I just *love* chat rooms.' She leaned forward and winked at him. 'I bet you didn't know there was a chat room for the over-eighties.'

Conner started to laugh. 'No, Mrs Patterson. I didn't know that. Do you party?'

'Like you wouldn't believe.' Her smile faded. 'But these eyes of mine...'

'Yes.' He shook his head and stood up. 'All right, let's take a look, although why I would want to fix your problem just so that you can spy on me, I don't know. It's probably dry-eye syndrome. You're spending too long on the computer. And that's something I've never had to say to an eighty-six-year-old before.'

'So, which young lady's heart are you breaking at the moment, you bad boy?'

Conner stilled, thinking of Flora. 'No one. I'm being boringly good.'

'You mean you don't want to tell me.' Agatha gave him a conspiratorial wink. 'That's good. When you care about a girl's reputation, it means it's serious.'

Conner stared at her. *Serious?* 'Trust me, Agatha, it isn't serious.'

'Ah—so there is someone.'

Realising that he'd just been outmanoeuvred by an eighty-six-year-old woman, Conner gave a silent laugh and examined her eyes, trying not to remember how Flora had looked when he'd said that she didn't turn him on.

Why on earth had she believed him?

Hadn't she seen that his words and his body had contradicted each other?

Apparently not, which just proved how naïve she was.

And proved that he'd been right to walk away.

He was absolutely *not* the man for her.

'Is everything all right?' Agatha looked at him anxiously. 'You seem very grim-faced.'

'I'm fine. Everything is fine.'

And it should have been.

He'd ended a completely unsuitable relationship before it had started. He should have been feeling good about himself. But he was experiencing his first ever attack of conscience.

He'd hurt women before. Plenty of them. And it had never particularly bothered him. He'd always thought it more cruel to let a woman delude herself and spend hours waiting by the phone for a call that wasn't going to come.

Fast and sharp, that's how he would have wanted it, so that's how he'd delivered it.

The difference was that he wasn't doing this for himself. He was doing it for Flora and there was a certain irony in the fact that his first truly unselfish act was causing her pain. And he was in agony.

Suddenly realising that Agatha was watching him closely, he pulled himself together. 'Do you have the central heating on at home?'

'Of course. This is Glenmore.' Her tone was dry. 'Without central heating I'd be too cold to sit at the computer.'

'Try logging on to somewhere warm,' he drawled, examining her eyes carefully. 'Mauritius is nice at this time of year. Central heating can make the irritation and redness a little worse. Tear secretion does reduce with age, Mrs Patterson.'

'So do all the other secretions, Dr MacNeil.' She gave him a saucy wink and Conner shook his head and started to laugh.

'I can't believe we're having this conversation. What were you like at twenty, Agatha?'

'I would have given you a run for your money, that's for sure.' She leaned forward, a twinkle in her eyes. 'You wouldn't have been able to walk away from that beach after a night with me.'

'I have no trouble believing you. All right, this is what we're going to do. I'm going to start by giving you artificial tears to use. It they don't make a difference, I can refer you to an ophthalmologist on the mainland for an opinion.'

'Can I contact him by email?'

Conner grinned and sat back down in his chair. 'I'm sure he'd be delighted to hear from you. Try the drops first. They might do the trick.' He studied his computer screen, clicked on the drug he wanted and printed off a prescription.

'You're a handsome one, aren't you?' Agatha gave a cheeky smile. 'If I'd seen you sixty years ago, you wouldn't have stood a chance.'

'Now, that's a pick-up line I haven't heard before.' Conner took the prescription out of the printer and stood up. 'Try these. If you have no joy, come back to me.'

'I certainly will.' She took the prescription, folded it and tucked it into her handbag. Then she stood up. 'The beach is still nice, you know. If you fancied paying a visit.'

Conner laughed. 'Get out of here, Agatha.'

'I'm going. I'm going.' And she left the room with slightly more bounce and energy than she'd shown when she'd entered it.

Flora began to wish that Glenmore was larger and busier. After her last humiliating encounter with Conner she was the one avoiding him, if such a thing was possible on an island as small as this one.

She arrived at work, hurried to her consulting room and then straight out on her calls. She didn't spend time in the staffroom and if she needed a doctor's advice on a patient, she sought out Logan.

It should have helped, but it didn't. She felt dreadful.

On the outside she looked as she always had—a little paler perhaps, but pretty much the same. But on the inside…on the inside she was ripped to shreds. She was *mortified* that she'd misinterpreted his actions and felt foolish beyond words for ever believing that a woman like her—*boring Flora*—could ever be attractive to a man like Conner.

He was a woman's dream, wasn't he?

She might be relatively inexperienced, but she wasn't blind. Women's eyes followed him wherever he went. That wicked, careless streak that defied the opinion of society was one of the very things that made him so appealing. He was his own person. As strong of mind as he was of body.

And she had to put him out of *her* mind and move on.

So she concentrated on work and succeeded in avoiding contact with him until one afternoon a thirteen-year-old boy with a cheeky smile and long, lanky limbs tapped on her door.

Recognising him immediately, Flora waved a hand towards the empty chair. 'Hi, Fraser, come on in. How are the summer holidays going?'

'Too fast.' The boy gave a shrug and stood awkwardly just inside the door.

Aisla, his mother, gave him a gentle push towards the chair. 'For goodness' sake, she isn't going to bite you!' She rolled her eyes at Flora. 'Honestly, these teenagers. They're men one minute and boys the next. He's terrified you're going to tell him to undress.'

Fraser shot his mother a horrified look, gave a grunt of embarrassment and slunk into the chair.

Flora smiled at him. 'What's the problem, Fraser?'

'It's my legs. Well, this leg mostly.' He stuck it out in front of him and frowned down at the mud and the bruises. 'I was doing football camp up at the school but I've had to stop.'

'Both the doctors are fully booked but Janet said you'd take a look and decide what we need to do,' Aisla said quickly. 'I don't know whether he needs an X-ray or what.'

'Did something happen? Did you fall?'

'I fall all the time. It's part of football.' Fraser rubbed his leg and Aisla gave a long-suffering sigh.

'I can vouch for that. You should see the colour of his clothes. I swear that all the mud of Glenmore is in my washing machine.'

Flora smiled and dropped to her knees beside Fraser. 'Let me take a look—show me exactly where it hurts. Here?'

'Ow!' Fraser winced. 'Right there. Have I broken it?'

'No, I don't think so. Nothing like that. I'm going to ask Logan to take a quick look.'

'Don't waste your time. He's just gone on a home visit,' Aisla told her wearily. 'We were in Reception when Janet took the call and he came rushing out. Some tourist with chest pain on the beach.'

'Oh.' Flora's heart rate trebled. 'Well, we could wait until he's back, I suppose. He might not be long.'

'I want to see Conner,' Fraser blurted out. 'He knows everything about football. Can we ask him to look at my leg?'

Just the sound of his name made her palms damp. 'With Logan out, he'll be very busy.'

'Is it worth just trying? Perhaps he'd see Fraser if you ask him.' Aisla's expression was worried. 'It's just that, if he thinks it should be X-rayed, I'm going to need to make some plans.'

'Of course I'll try. Wait there a moment.' Hoping she didn't look as reluctant as she felt, Flora left her room and took several deep breaths. Across the corridor a patient left Conner's room and Flora felt her knees turn to liquid.

She couldn't do it. She really couldn't face him.

She turned backwards to her room and then realised that she couldn't do that either. How could she tell Aisla that she was too pathetic to face Conner?

Taking a deep breath, she walked briskly over to his door and rapped hard, before she could change her mind.

Keep it brief and to the point, she told herself. Professional. And don't look at him. *Whatever you do, don't look at him.*

'Yes?' The harsh bark of his voice made her jump and she wondered how any of the patients ever plucked up courage to go and see him. Closing her eyes briefly, she took a deep breath and opened the door.

'I just wanted to ask if you'd see a patient for me. Thirteen-year-old boy complaining of pain in his leg. It's tender and there's swelling over the tibial tubercle.' She adjusted her glasses, still not looking at him. 'He's been at football camp so it's possible that he's injured himself, but I'm wondering whether it could be Osgood-Schlatter disease.'

'Reading all those books has obviously paid off.'

She had the feeling that he was intentionally trying to hurt her and she didn't understand it. He wasn't unkind, she knew he wasn't. Why would he want to hurt her? 'Obviously I'm not qualified to make that diagnosis.' Suffering agonies of embarrassment, she cleared her throat. 'He's in my room now. He's suffering from an attack of hero-worship and is desperate for your opinion on his leg.'

'Ah…' He spoke softly. 'Patient pressure. And I'm willing to bet you tried Logan first.'

'Fraser is Logan's patient so he was the logical first choice.'

'And nowhere near as terrifying as facing me. How much courage did it take for you to knock on my door?'

She stiffened. 'Please, don't make fun of me, Dr MacNeil.'

'Do I look as though I'm laughing?' With a low growl of impatience, he rose to his feet. 'There are things I need to say to you, Flora.'

'You made your thoughts perfectly clear the last time we spoke. If you could just see the patient and give me your opinion, I can take it from there.' Terrified that she was about to make a fool of herself, Flora turned and walked quickly back to her room, her heart thundering in her chest. Aware that Conner was right behind her, she concentrated on Fraser. 'Dr MacNeil will take a look at you, Fraser.'

Conner threw her a dark and dangerous look that promised trouble for the next time they were alone. 'Can you lie on the couch, Fraser? I want to examine you properly.' He waited as Fraser winced and limped to the couch and then examined the boy, his hands gentle.

'It's not my hip, it's my leg,' Fraser muttered as Conner examined his joints.

'But your hip is attached to your leg,' Conner observed in a mild tone, 'so sometimes a problem with one can cause a pain in the other. Does this hurt?'

'No.'

'This?'

'Ow! Yes, yes.' Fraser swore and his mother gasped in shock and embarrassment.

'Fraser Price, you watch your language! Where did you learn that?'

'Everyone says it,' Fraser mumbled. 'It's no big deal.'

'It's a big deal to me!'

'I bet Conner swore when he was my age.'

'He's Dr MacNeil to you,' Aisla said sharply, and Conner cleared his throat tactfully and examined the other hip.

'I can't remember that far back. Is this OK? I'm going to bend your knee now—good. Do you play a lot of sport?'

'Yes, all the time. Just like you did.' Fraser grinned. 'Football, beach volleyball, loads of different stuff.'

It wasn't just the women who adored him, Flora thought helplessly, *it was the children, too.* They thought he was *so* cool.

Aisla looked at Conner. 'Do you think we need to have it X-rayed?'

'No.' Conner straightened. 'You can sit up now, Fraser. I'm done. As Nurse Harris correctly assessed, you have something called Osgood-Schlatter disease. It's a condition that sometimes affects athletic teenagers, particularly boys. There's inflammation and swelling at the top end of the tibia—here.' He took Fraser's hand and placed it on his leg. 'Can you feel it?'

'Yes.' Fraser winced. 'So will it go away?'

'Eventually. But you're going to need to play a bit less football.'

'How much less?'

'You need to cut down on your physical activity, because that will only make things worse.'

'All of it? Everything I do?' Fraser sounded appalled and Conner put a hand on his shoulder.

'It's tough, I know. But basically you need to stop doing anything that aggravates your condition. Ideally you should avoid sport altogether until your bones have fully matured, but I appreciate that's asking a bit much. A compromise would be to stop if you feel that whatever you're doing is making it worse.' He glanced at Aisla. 'He can take anti-inflammatories for the pain. If it doesn't improve, we can immobilise it for a short time and see if that helps. Failing that, we can refer him to an orthopaedic consultant for an assessment.'

Fraser slumped. 'No football?'

'Try cutting back. That will allow the pain and swelling to resolve. Anything that makes it worse, stop doing it.'

'Will it go?'

'Once your bones have fully matured. Unfortunately, the more active you are, the worse the symptoms are likely to be.'

Fraser looked grumpy. 'I'll have to spend the summer playing on game machines.'

'I don't think so,' his mother said dryly. 'You can read a few books.'

'Books!' Fraser's face went from grumpy to mournful. 'It's my holiday! Why would I want to spend it staring at a book?'

Aisla walked towards the door. 'Thanks, Dr MacNeil. Flora. We're grateful.'

Conner waited for the door to close behind him. 'I don't know which upset him more—the prospect of cutting back on football or the thought of reading books.'

'It was a close-run thing.' Careful not to look at him, Flora changed the paper on the couch. 'Thank you for seeing him.'

'Your diagnosis was correct. Well done. That was very impressive.'

'Thank you. I'm pleased all that studying paid off.' Although she didn't look at him, she knew he was watching her. She could feel him watching her.

'Flora…' His voice was husky. 'I know you're hurt and I'm sorry.'

'I thought you never apologised.'

'Well I'm apologising now,' he said testily, and she shrugged.

'You don't have to apologise for not finding me attractive,' Flora said stiffly, and heard him inhale sharply.

'I know you won't believe me, but I was doing you a favour.'

'Really? It's doing me a favour to kiss me and then tell me I'm boring?'

'I should never have kissed you in the first place.'

'So why did you?' She breathed in and out, forcing air into

her lungs. 'Not once, but twice. The kiss on the beach—all right, let's say that was an accident. But you kissed me again, didn't you? If I'm so boring, why did you do that? Were you just teasing me? Doing me a favour, giving boring old Flora a thrill? Did you just do it to hurt my feelings? It was patronizing, Conner. You made me— I was…' She couldn't even say the words. 'If you didn't want me then you should have just left me alone. Or are you so bad that you just have to cause hurt?'

'Bad? You think I'm bad?' He pressed her against the wall, his body hard against hers. 'I'll show you what bad is, Flora.' He brought his mouth down on hers with punishing force, kissing her with raw, explosive passion, the slide of his tongue explicitly sexual and unbelievably seductive.

And she melted. Her head spinning from his skilled assault on her senses, she kissed him back, feeling fire dance inside her belly. She wasn't capable of thought or speech—all she could do was respond to his demands. She did so willingly and when he finally lifted his head she stared at him, mute.

'I've been called bad by a lot of people,' he said hoarsely, his hands planted either side of her head so that she couldn't escape his gaze, 'and most of it has been justified. But I'm damned if I'm accepting that criticism when it comes to you, Flora Harris. If I was as bad as people think, we would have already had sex.'

She was dizzy with need, unable to make sense of what he was saying. 'But you don't find me attractive.'

'No?' He slid his hands over her bottom and pulled her into him so that she felt the hard ridge of his arousal pressing against her. 'What I really want to do right now is strip you naked and take you hard and fast until we're both so exhausted that neither of us can move. And then I want to do it again. And again. Do you understand me?'

She gave a little whimper of shock and his eyes darkened. 'I'm not talking about marriage, or friendship or any of

those soft, woolly things. I'm talking about sex, Flora. Sex.'
He released her suddenly and took a step backwards, a look of
disgust on his face. 'And that isn't the sort of person you are,
which is why I'm going to let you go now. I'm going to walk
out of that door into my consulting room and you're not going
to follow me. You are a woman who deserves a conventional
relationship with a reliable guy. I'm neither of those things.'

She licked her lips, shaken by everything he'd said to her.
'I don't think you should tell me what I want.'

'You're too naïve to play this game.'

'I am not naïve. I'm not naïve, Conner.' There was tearing
agony inside her. *He was going to walk away from her again.*
'Would it make a difference if I told you that I'm not a virgin?
Is that what's worrying you?'

He inhaled sharply and turned away, his profile tense.
'Don't tell me that.'

'I just thought it might make a difference.'

A muscle worked in his cheek. 'It doesn't. And you might
find this hard to believe, but the desire *not* to hurt you is the
reason I walked away. And it's the reason I'm about to walk
away again. Because there are some rules that even I won't
break.' He ran a hand over his face and then strode out of the
room, leaving her shaking so badly that she could hardly stand.

He wanted her?

She sank onto her chair, staring at the door. He'd pulled back
out of consideration for her? He didn't find her repulsive?

She wasn't 'boring Flora'?

Her fragile, bruised confidence recovered slightly and her
mind started to race.

CHAPTER EIGHT

CONNER lay sprawled on the huge sofa in the barn, mindlessly flicking through the sports channels on the television. On the floor next to him was a bottle of whisky and a half-filled glass. He stared at it blankly and was just about to pick up the bottle and do what needed to be done when someone hammered hard on the front door.

Conner reached for the remote control and increased the volume on the television, determined to ignore whoever it was who mistakenly believed that he might be in need of company.

There was no second knock, so he picked up the whisky bottle, satisfied that his unwelcome visitor had decided to go and bother someone else.

He stared at the television screen for a moment, too emotionally drained to find an alternative mode of entertainment. After a few moments some deep-seated instinct warned him that he wasn't alone and he turned his head slowly.

Flora stood in the doorway.

She was wearing a coat belted at the waist and raindrops glistened like diamonds on her dark hair. 'You didn't answer your door.'

Whisky sloshed over his shirt and it took him a moment to reply, the speed of his mind and his tongue dulled by the shock of seeing her there. 'I didn't feel like company.'

'Well, that's tough because there are things I need to say to you.' She stepped into the room, her eyes burning with a fire that he'd never seen before. 'That was quite a speech you made earlier, Conner MacNeil. You said a lot of things.'

What was she doing here? 'They were things that needed saying.'

'I agree. And I've been thinking about those things.' She breathed in and out, her chest rising and falling under her raincoat. 'You've made a lot of assumptions about me.' Water clung to her eyelashes and cheeks and her hair, as dark as mahogany, curled around her face. She looked pretty and wholesome and he had to force himself not to look at her soft mouth.

If he looked, he was lost.

'You shouldn't be here, Flora.'

Her eyes slid to the whisky bottle. 'Oh, Conner…' Her gentle, sympathetic tone scratched against his nerve endings.

'Go home.'

'Why? Because you're drunk?'

He licked his lips and discovered they were dry. 'I'm not drunk.'

But she didn't seem to be listening. It was as if she was in the middle of a rehearsed speech. 'You're worried in case you lose control and behave badly?' She stepped closer, the blaze in her eyes intensifying. 'What would you say if I told you that I *want* you to behave badly, Conner? In fact, I want you to be as bad as you can possibly be.'

The breath hissed through his teeth. 'For God's sake, Flora…'

'People say you're super-bright. Shockingly intelligent— brain in a different stratosphere to most people's, and all that. I'm not sure if they're right or not. What I do know is that you're certainly very slow when it comes to knowing what I want.'

His hand tightened around the glass. 'I said, *go home*!'

'Why? So that you can get slowly drunk on your own? I don't think that's the answer.'

'Well, you wouldn't, would you?' He gave a mocking smile. 'I'm willing to bet you've never been drunk in your life, Flora Harris.'

'You're right, actually. I haven't.' Her tone was calm. 'I never saw the point. There are other ways to solve a problem.'

'What makes you think I'm solving a problem?'

Her eyes flickered to the bottle. 'If you're not solving a problem, why are you drinking?'

'Actually, I'm not drinking.'

But she still wasn't listening. 'I don't know what you're searching for but you won't find it in the bottom of a whisky bottle.'

He gave a cynical smile. 'My father did.'

'You're not your father, Conner.' She spoke quietly. 'Which is why I'm standing here now.' She let the coat slip from her shoulders and underneath she was naked apart from the skimpiest, sexiest underwear he'd ever seen. 'You think I'm a good girl, Conner? You think you're not allowed to touch me?'

The glass slipped from his hand and the whisky spilled over the floor. Conner didn't notice because every neurone in his brain had fused.

Her body was all smooth lines and delicate curves, her legs impossibly long and her small breasts pressing against the filmy lace of her bra.

He stared at her in tense silence. 'I didn't think I'd drunk anything,' he muttered to himself in a hoarse voice, 'but perhaps I'm wrong about that. For a moment there I thought Flora Harris was standing in front of me in her underwear.'

She made an exasperated sound and removed the bottle from his hand. 'You've had enough.' Her subtle, floral perfume drifted towards him and he leaned his head back against the sofa with a groan.

'Believe me, I haven't had enough. I haven't even started.

But if I'm still imagining Flora naked, perhaps it's time I did. I need the image to fade to black.'

'It won't fade because it's real. *I'm* real. Oh, for goodness' sake, Conner, I came here to seduce you and you're—you're…' She sighed with frustration and put the bottle on the floor, spilling some of the contents in the process. 'Why did you open a bottle of whisky?'

'Because of you.'

'Me? *I'm* the reason you're drunk?'

'I'm not drunk. But for a brief moment it seemed like a good idea. I thought it might take my mind off ravishing you,' he mumbled, and she made a sound that was somewhere between a moan and a giggle.

'Why do you need to do that? I *want* you to ravish me. I'm desperate for you to ravish me.'

He squinted up at her. 'Am I dreaming?'

'No, you're not dreaming!' She gave a sigh and shook her head. 'You're going to take a cold shower and while you're doing that I'm going to make you a jug of very strong coffee.'

Conner rubbed his eyes with the tips of his fingers and shook his head. 'You don't need to do that. And coffee stops me sleeping.'

'Good.' She sounded more exasperated than ever. 'I don't want you sleeping. I want you awake when I seduce you. I've spent most of my life listening to other women telling me what an amazing lover you are, and just when I'm about to find out what all the fuss is about, you pass out on me.'

'I'm not going to pass out.'

'Get in that shower, Conner MacNeil, or I swear I'll throw a bucket of freezing water over you right here!'

He ran a tongue over his lips. 'You look like Flora but you're not acting like Flora. Flora never swears. She's a really sweet girl.'

'Sweet? I'll show you sweet.' She grabbed his arm and yanked. 'Stand up! You're too heavy for me to pull you.'

He wondered if she'd be as confident if she knew he was as sober as she was.

Aware that his body was betraying his emotions in the most visible way possible, Conner stood up and gave a wry smile. 'I spilt half the bottle over myself when you walked through the door, so a shower might be a good idea. A freezing one, to kill my libido.'

'I don't want you to kill your libido.' Her voice was sultry and she pulled him against her and stood on tiptoe. 'Kiss me, Conner. And then go and take that shower. I want you sober enough to remember this. I don't want to wake up tomorrow and have you mouthing all sorts of excuses about being too drunk to know what you were doing.'

He knew exactly what he was doing and it felt incredible.

He groaned as he felt her silky smooth body pressing against his. He just couldn't help himself and he brought his mouth down on hers, stars exploding in his head as her tongue met his. 'You taste fantastic.'

She pulled away from him, her eyes soft and her cheeks pink. 'Where's your bathroom?'

'I don't need a cold shower.'

'Yes, you do.'

'Where is Flora? I think you've hit her on the head and stolen her identity.' He ran a hand through his hair as she tugged him towards the bathroom and hit a button on the shower. 'Flora isn't a forceful woman.'

'There's lots you don't know about Flora.'

He was starting to agree with her, especially when she reached up and yanked impatiently at his shirt, scattering buttons around the bathroom floor. Then he felt her fingers slide into the waistband of his jeans.

His hands covered hers and he gave her a sexy smile, astonished and delighted by her new-found confidence. 'Careful, angel. That's the danger zone and Flora would never wander into the danger zone.'

She gave him a gentle push and he swore fluently and then sucked in a breath as freezing water sluiced over his back. '*That* is cold.'

'Good—it's supposed to be cold. Stay in there until you can walk in a straight line unaided and tell me your name and date of birth. I'll be in the kitchen when you're ready.'

Her hand shaking, Flora rummaged through his fridge and found a packet of fresh coffee. She spooned a generous quantity into a cafetière and topped it up with hot water.

Then she sat at the table, listening to the rushing sound of the shower.

He was taking a long time.

Was it safe to have left him there? Had he drowned?

Or maybe she'd totally misread the situation and he was spending a long time in there in the hope that she'd give up and go home.

Her nerve faltered and she caught her lower lip between her teeth.

What on earth did she think she was doing?

He was absolutely right. She wasn't the sort of woman who stripped off and issued invitations to men. Neither was she the sort of woman who made coffee for a man while dressed in silk underwear.

With a whimper of panic she was just about to sprint back into the sitting room and retrieve her coat, when he walked into the kitchen. He'd knotted a towel around his waist but droplets of water still clung to the dark tangle of curls that shadowed his chest. His shoulders were broad and powerful and his arms strong and muscular. He had a body designed to make a woman think of nothing but sin, but what really caught her attention was the look in his eyes. Lazy, sexy and ready for action.

Her nerve fled completely and she decided to follow. 'Coffee on the table,' she muttered as she backed towards the door.

A hand shot out and closed around her wrist, his fingers like bands of steel as he yanked her back towards him. 'Oh, no, you don't.' His voice was cool and rock steady. 'You told me to shower. I've showered.'

'You can't possibly have sobered up that quickly.'

'I was never drunk.'

She stared at him. 'I saw the bottle.'

'I admit I considered it. That's how low I felt.' His eyes held hers for a long moment. 'But if there's one thing that being around my father taught me, it's that drink solves nothing. I was about to pour it down the sink when you walked in.'

'You smelt of alcohol.'

His smile was faintly mocking. 'When you took your coat off, I spilled most of it.'

Her heart thumped as she re-examined the facts. He hadn't been drunk. He'd been sober. She swallowed hard, all her courage leaving her. Somehow her belief that he was drunk had made him less intimidating and now, knowing that he hadn't touched a drop, she felt suddenly shaky.

'I should probably leave now. I've just remembered that I—'

'What?' His mouth was dangerously close to hers, his tone low and impossibly sexy as he curved an arm around her waist and trapped her against him. 'What have you just remembered, Flora?'

She could hardly breathe. 'Flora? Who's she? Oh, I remember—she's the woman I left her locked in her cottage when I stole her identity. I need to go and let her out.'

He gave a slow smile and his head lowered towards hers. 'Too late, sweetheart.' He paused, his mouth tantalisingly close to hers, 'You are most definitely Flora. A whole new Flora. A standing-naked-in-my-kitchen Flora.'

'In my underwear…'

His lips brushed hers, a deliberately erotic hint of things to come. He gave a low, appreciative murmur. 'You taste good.

Whatever happens in the next few hours, don't dig your fingernails into my shoulders. If this is a dream, I don't want to be woken up.'

Her entire body was throbbing but still the nerves fluttered in her stomach. He was so sure and confident, whereas she… 'I made you coffee.'

'I don't want it.' His mouth slid down her neck and lingered at the base of her throat, his tongue tasting her skin. 'I want you, sweetheart.'

Her pulse was thundering and she tilted her head back with a gasp. 'Conner…'

'You came here to seduce me…' His lips moved slowly along her shoulder. 'You want to know what sort of lover I am.'

As she felt his hands slide confidently down her back, she gave a shiver. 'I thought you didn't find me attractive.'

'I always found you attractive. But you were always off limits as far as I was concerned. Despite what everyone thought of me, that was the one line I was never prepared to cross.'

'But you're crossing it now.'

'No. *You're* crossing it.' He lifted his head and looked down at her, his ice-blue eyes compelling. 'This was your decision, Flora. You made it by coming here.'

He was giving her the chance to change her mind. But she didn't want to do that. 'Yes.'

'So…' His hand slid slowly down her back and cupped her bottom. 'You came here to seduce me.'

She couldn't breathe. 'Yes.'

He gave a slow smile. 'Carry on, angel. I'm all yours.'

Was that it? *Was that all the help he was going to give her?* For a moment her courage faltered but then she looked at his gorgeous naked body and couldn't help herself. She leaned forward and pressed her mouth to his chest, while her fingers trailed slowly across the hard muscle of his abdomen and lower still until they brushed against the top of the towel that was all that was between her and his straining manhood.

'All right, commercial break,' he said roughly, scooping her up into his arms as if she weighed nothing, 'If you carry on like that, this whole event is going to be very short-lived. You need to slow things down, angel. Make me beg.'

Beg?

She had no idea how to make a man beg. Flora clamped her mouth shut, judging it wise not to confess as much at this point. The problem with playing the seductress was that you were expected to follow through.

He carried her up a flight of stairs to the bedroom. Dusk was falling but there was enough light for her to see open fields and the jagged ruins of Glenmore Castle.

'It's a wonderful view,' she breathed, and he gave a lazy, confident smile as he deposited her in the centre of the bed.

'The only view you're going to be looking at has me in it.' He delivered a lingering kiss to her mouth and then lay down beside her and rolled onto his back, arrogantly sure of himself, his gaze direct.

And she understood. He wanted active, not passive. He was giving her the chance to change her mind but she had no intention of doing that.

She wanted this. *She wanted him.* And this time she wasn't going to blow it. The whole of Glenmore could sing and dance outside his bedroom window and it wouldn't make any difference.

Aware that he was waiting for her to make the first move, she reached out a hand and stroked his shoulder, shivering slightly as she felt smooth skin and powerful male muscle.

He lay still, his eyelids lowered, watching and waiting, and suddenly she felt desperately nervous and impossibly excited.

'You can stop whenever you want,' he murmured, but he sounded less cool and composed than usual and the edgy quality to his voice gave her courage.

'I'm not stopping. You have an amazing body,' she said huskily, and her eyes slid shyly to his and her insides tumbled and warmed. He was so outrageously sexy that it was hard not to stare and even harder not to touch. She leaned forward and kissed his cheek, feeling the roughness of male stubble under her lips. Then she ran a finger over his nose, exploring the bump. 'How did you break it? Were you fighting?'

'Rugby.' He turned his head and kissed her fingers. 'I'm not quite the animal everyone seems to think I am.'

'Aren't you?' She trailed her finger over his mouth and then replaced it with her lips and he slid a hand behind her head and held her there while they kissed. His mouth was hot and purposeful and she felt the excitement flash through her body, turning her from willing to desperate.

Her hand slid over his shoulder, tracing flesh and hard muscle, and then lowered her head and rubbed her cheek over the roughness of his chest and breathed in his erotic scent. Her hand lingered low on his abdomen and she felt his muscles clench in an involuntary response.

She allowed her fingers to linger in that dangerous place, teasing and promising, and then she bent her head and kissed his shoulder, using lips and tongue to discover and explore his body, gradually moving lower until her mouth rested where her hand had been. His muscles quivered under her gentle touch and she heard the sharp hiss of his breath as she teased him with her tongue. He sank his fingers into her hair and then released her instantly. She glanced up at him and saw that his eyes were closed and his jaw was clenched. Desire burned deep inside her and she bent her head again and closed her mouth over him and he made a choking sound.

'Flora...'

She lifted her head. 'Sorry—am I hurting you? Your face is sort of...twisted.'

'You're not hurting me,' he said hoarsely, 'but—'

'Good.' She lowered her head again and used her tongue and her lips until he gave a harsh groan, grabbed her and rolled her onto her back.

'You have to stop. I'm not going to last five minutes if you…' He closed his eyes and breathed deeply, tension etched in every line of his handsome face. 'Give me a minute. Just give me a minute.'

'Did I do something wrong?' She was suddenly covered with embarrassment. 'I—I haven't actually done it before…'

He shifted so that he was half on top of her, one leg pinning her to the mattress. 'You're full of surprises, do you know that? If you've never actually done it before, where did you—?' His voice cracked and he cleared his throat. 'Learn those tricks?'

'From a book.'

'A book?' He gave a shaky laugh. 'A book. Typical Flora.' He bent his head and kissed her mouth expertly and her body trembled and ached in response.

And he hadn't even touched her yet.

Desperate for him to do so, her hips moved against him and he put a hand on her hip to steady her. Only then did she realise that at some point he'd removed her underwear. And she hadn't even noticed. She was about to ask him about it when he lowered his head and drew her nipple into his mouth.

Sensation shot through her and she tried to move against him, but he held her firmly while he lavished attention on both her breasts. The pleasure was so intense it was almost unbearable, and when he finally lifted his head, her cheeks were flushed and her limbs were trembling. For a moment he just looked at her and she thought that she was going to be the one to beg, and then she felt his hand between her thighs and the expert stroke of his fingers as they discovered the heart of her.

His touch was so intimate that for a moment she stiffened and instantly felt him pause. And the fact that he'd paused made her realise just how much care he was taking with her.

'Conner—please— I don't think I can wait.'

With a skilled, knowing fingers he found exactly the right place and caressed her gently until the excitement grew from a slow ache to a maddening turmoil of sensation. As his exploration grew bolder and more intimate, she arched and writhed, silently begging for the possession that her body craved.

'Look at me, Flora.' He shifted over her, slid a hand under her bottom and she felt the blunt tip of his erection brushing against her. For a moment she couldn't breathe, the excitement and anticipation so great that her entire body was trembling with need. And then he eased forward slowly and she gasped because it took her body a moment to accommodate him.

He paused, his breath warming her neck. 'Am I hurting you?'

'No.'

'Relax, angel.' He closed his mouth over hers, kissed her deeply and moved forward, driving deeper inside her. 'Relax for me.'

But she didn't want to relax. She wanted— *She wanted...*

Excitement exploded inside her and she rose instinctively to meet his thrusts.

Her heart thudded wildly and she curved her hands over his bottom, urging him on. 'Conner, Conner...' She looked into his eyes and saw primitive need blazing there.

He slowed the pace, his eyes holding hers. 'Are you OK?'

'Yes...' Talking was difficult. 'It's just that you look—' She broke off and moaned as he moved again in an agonisingly slow rhythm.

'How do I look?'

'Sort of—scary.'

'I'm trying not to lose control.' He gave a wry smile. 'And it's pretty hard.'

'Then stop trying.' She breathed the words against his mouth and felt him tense. 'I'm not delicate, Conner. Make love to me the way you want to make love to me.'

His eyes darkened and his breathing quickened. 'I never want to hurt you, Flora.'

'You won't hurt me.' But the fact that he cared enough to be careful with her increased the feeling of warmth growing inside her. 'I'm OK. I've never been so OK,' she murmured, and his mouth flickered into a half-smile and he surged into her again, this time going deeper.

And she felt the change in him. He shifted his position, altered the rhythm, and her body hummed and fizzled and then tightened around his in an explosion of ecstasy so intense that it drove him to his own completion.

Flora lay in his arms, stunned and breathless. 'I—I had no idea that it would be like that.'

He turned his head, a frown on his face. 'You told me you weren't a virgin.'

'Technically I wasn't.' Her voice was soft and her eyes were misty. 'But I suppose it depends on your definition. I've never done that before. Never felt like that before.'

'I don't think I want to hear about your past lovers.' He folded her back against him in a possessive gesture and she smiled, feeling warm and protected and—just amazing.

'Lover. Just the one.'

'I definitely don't want to hear this,' Conner muttered darkly. 'Knowing you, it must have been serious.'

'I suppose it was a serious attempt to discover what all the fuss was about. He was a lawyer—very proper. Predictable. Chivalrous.'

'All the things I'm not.' Conner's arms tightened. 'He sounds like the perfect mate. You should have stuck with him.'

She lay in the semi-darkness, staring at his profile, thinking of the care he'd taken with her. 'I didn't love him.'

'Oh, please.' He made an impatient sound and she turned her head.

'It's true. I know you don't believe in love, but I do. And I didn't love him. My feelings just weren't right. There was no chemistry.' She gave a short laugh. 'That's what you said to me.'

'I was lying.' Conner bent his head and kissed her. 'And if

you weren't so naïve, you would have known I was lying, because I had a massive erection as I said it.'

She gasped and then gave a strangled laugh. 'Conner MacNeil, why must you always try and shock?'

'The fact that you're shocked proves my point. You're naïve.'

'I'm *not* naïve. And it's hardly surprising that I didn't notice anything because I was so upset, I was trying not to look at you. And it wasn't hard to believe you when you said I didn't turn you on, because I know I'm not sexy.'

It was Conner's turn to laugh. 'Angel, if you were any sexier you'd have to carry a government health warning.'

She slid her arm over his stomach and rested her chin on his chest. 'Really?'

'You need to ask?' He guided her hand down his body and gave her a wicked smile. 'You currently have a hold on the evidence.'

She smiled. 'Do you know what's amazing? I don't feel at all shy with you.'

'I'd noticed. Permit me to say that your behaviour tonight would have thoroughly shocked the inhabitants of Glenmore.'

'I don't care about them,' she said honestly, and he stroked her hair away from her face, his expression serious.

'Yes, you do, and I don't blame you for that. Glenmore is your home. Talking of which…' He frowned suddenly and then released her and sprang out of bed. 'Where did you park?'

'Sorry?'

'Your car. Where did you park your car?'

She frowned. 'Outside your barn. Where else?'

'Someone could see it.' He reached down and pulled her gently to her feet. 'You have to leave, angel.'

'Now?' Bemused, she slid her arms around his neck. 'I—I assumed I'd stay the night.'

'At least eight islanders drive past my barn on the way to work in the morning. I don't want them seeing your car.' He gently unhooked her arms from his neck and retrieved her underwear from the floor. 'You need to leave, Flora.'

His words made her feel sick and her heart bumped uncomfortably. 'So—that's it?'

He slid her arms into her bra and fastened it with as much skill as he'd shown unfastening it. 'No, of course that's not it.' He lowered his head and kissed her swiftly. 'Are you busy tomorrow night?'

'No.'

He smiled and winked at her. 'Then you can cook me dinner. Meet me here at eight o'clock.' Then he frowned. 'On second thoughts, your place is probably better. Evanna's cottage is off the main road.'

She felt a rush of excitement and anticipation but tried to hide it. 'Why can't *you* cook *me* dinner?'

'Because I'm rubbish in the kitchen and I'm assuming you'd rather not be poisoned,' he drawled, sliding her silk knickers up her legs and then giving a tormented groan. 'Why am I dressing you when all I want to do is *un*dress you?'

'I don't know,' she said breathlessly. 'Why are you?'

'Because I care about you. I care about your reputation.'

She looked at him curiously. 'That doesn't exactly sound like Bad Conner.'

'You've corrupted me,' he said roughly. And then he took a deep breath, stepped back and lifted his hands. 'Get out of here. Your coat is downstairs. For goodness' sake, remember to button it or you'll give everyone a cheap thrill. Go, quickly, before I change my mind.'

CHAPTER NINE

FLORA tried, she *really* tried, to keep their relationship secret. She made a point of not gazing at him when they were in public together and she kept their interaction brief and formal. But inside she trembled with insecurity when he didn't glance at her and she knew why.

No relationship of Conner's had ever lasted. Why should theirs be any different?

But even knowing that it was probably doomed, she wouldn't have changed anything. And if she spent her days racked with doubt as to his feelings, when night came she was left in no doubt at all.

Every evening he arrived at her cottage and spent time with her until the early hours. They ate, talked and made love, but he never stayed the whole night and Flora didn't know whether she felt frustrated by that or grateful.

On the one hand she was slightly relieved not to be the subject of local gossip, but on the other hand she was greedy for time with him. She loved the fact that he talked to her and sensed that he said things to her that he'd never said to anyone else.

Occasionally the conversation turned to the topic of his father. 'It's hardly any wonder you virtually lived wild,' she murmured one night as she lay with her head on his shoulder. 'I don't suppose there was much to go home to.'

'It wasn't exactly a laugh a minute.' He stroked a hand over her hair. 'After my mother left, he was pretty much drunk from the moment he woke up in the morning to the moment he keeled over at night. I stayed out of his way. Half the time I didn't even go home. I slept on the beach or borrowed the MacDonalds' barn. That was fine until the night I lit a fire to keep warm and the wind changed.'

Flora's heart twisted. 'I guessed things were bad. I went up there once, to look for you. And he yelled at me so violently that my legs shook for days.'

His arms tightened around her. 'Why were you looking for me?'

'After your mother left, I was worried about you. And I thought I understood what you were going through. How arrogant was that?' She sighed and kissed him gently. 'I suppose because I'd lost my mother, too, I thought I might be able to help you. But of course our situations were entirely different because I still had my dad.'

'I didn't want to be helped. I just wanted to be angry.'

'I don't blame you for being angry.' She rubbed her cheek against his shoulder. 'Was it the army that stopped you being angry?'

'They taught me to channel my aggression. Running thirty miles with a pack on your back pretty much wipes it out of you.'

'So they helped you?'

'Yes, I suppose they did.' He kissed the top of her head. 'You're such a gentle person, I don't suppose you've ever been angry.'

'Of course I have. Anger is a human emotion. But I didn't have reason to be angry—not like you. I feel so bad for you. The locals should have done something.'

'What could they have done? And, anyway, I didn't exactly invite assistance.'

'You basically grew up without parents.' She raised herself

on one elbow, her expression soft as she looked down at him. 'Why did you become a doctor?'

'I don't know.' His eyes closed again. 'I spent my whole life on Glenmore being angry. I suppose it was a bit of a vicious circle. They thought the worst of me so I gave them the worst. And then I left and suddenly I was with people who didn't know me. And I realised that I was tired of living my life like that. I went to an army recruitment day and it all happened from there.'

'Did you ever hear from your Dad?'

'No. And I never contacted him either.'

'But you kept in touch with Logan.'

Conner's eyes opened. 'Logan is a good man. Always was. He was the one who told me about my father's cirrhosis. He arranged for his admission to hospital on the mainland and he did all the paperwork when he died. Logan did all the things I should have done.' He hesitated. 'He was also the one who thought I should come back and tie up some loose ends. Sell the house, bury some ghosts—that sort of thing.'

'I'm glad you came back.'

He looked at her. 'I'm not good for you, Flora,' he murmured, stroking his hands over her hair and then pulling her down so that he could kiss her. 'I'm just going to hurt you.'

'I'll take that chance.'

'Relationships are destructive, terrible things.'

'I can understand why you'd think that, given everything that happened with your parents, but theirs was just one relationship, Conner. My parents' relationship was different.'

'Your mother died and your father was devastated,' he said softly. 'In its own way, that relationship was as traumatic as the one my parents had. Both ended in misery.'

'It was traumatic, that's true. But what my father and mother shared was so special that I know Dad wouldn't have changed things, even if he'd been able to foresee what was going to happen. True love is rare and special—a real gift. You don't turn that away, even if it comes with pain.'

'Love is a curse, Flora Harris, not a gift.'

'No, Conner.' She kissed him gently. 'The best thing that can happen to anyone is to be truly loved. Whatever happens in adult life, every child deserves to be loved unconditionally by their parents, and that didn't happen to you. And I'm guessing you haven't experienced it as an adult either, given the way you stomp through relationships.'

'Don't be so sure.' He lifted an eyebrow. 'Do you want to know how many women have told me that they love me?'

'Actually, I don't.' She laughed, trying to ignore the queasy feeling in her stomach that his words had induced. 'And I was talking about love, not sex.'

'All right, it's *definitely* time that you stopped talking.' He rolled her swiftly onto her back and came down on top of her, pinning her still with his weight. 'If the only thing on your mind is love, I'm going to have to do something brutal.' But his eyes were gentle and she giggled softly.

How did he feel about her?

How did she feel about him?

She really didn't know.

Their relationship was the most thrilling, exciting thing that had ever happened to her, but at the same time she knew that there couldn't be a happy ending.

But for the time being she was just going to live in the present.

And that was what she did.

But rumours were gradually spreading across Glenmore.

A few weeks into their relationship, Flora was in the pub with the rest of the medical centre staff, including an extremely pregnant Evanna.

'At the weekend I'm taking you over to the mainland.'

Logan raised his glass to his wife. 'That baby is going to come any time now.'

'No hurry.' Evanna glanced at Flora. 'Are you going to manage?'

'Of course.'

'Hey, Conner.' Jim wandered over to their table and slapped Conner on the shoulders. 'How are you doing?'

Flora studied her grapefruit juice intently, careful not to look at Conner.

'I'm good, Jim.' Conner leaned back in his chair and stretched his legs out under the table. 'And you?'

'Bit tired.' Jim winked at him. 'Woken up by that bike of yours at three in the morning every night this week. Thought to myself, Young Conner's been out on the hunt.'

Flora felt her face flame, but Conner simply stifled a yawn, apparently unflustered. 'Just relieving the boredom of being stuck on Glenmore, Jim. Do you blame me?'

'No, but I envy you.' Jim gave a delighted laugh. 'Go on, lad. Tell us the name of the lucky girl. Knowing you, it's someone different from the girl you were hiding in the waves the night we saw you on the beach.'

'Of course. That was weeks ago and I'm not into long relationships.' Conner didn't falter but Flora's breathing stopped and inside she suffered an agony of embarrassment.

People were talking. Of course they were. How could she have imagined otherwise?

How long would it take for people to put two and two together?

And how would she cope with being on the receiving end of everyone's nudges and winks?

This time *she'd* be the one that everyone was talking about when they bought their apples in the greengrocer on the quay. *She'd* be the subject of speculative glances when she took her books back to the library.

Flora tightened her fingers round her glass and tried to

breathe steadily and slow her heart rate, but inside she was shrinking because she knew only too well what they'd all be saying.

That Conner MacNeil had seduced her and that it wouldn't last five minutes.

She took a large slug of her drink and then realised that Conner was looking at her, his gaze curiously intent. Unable to look away, she slowly put her glass down on the table.

He gave a faint smile and something in that smile worried her. He looked…resigned? *Tired?*

She looked away quickly, telling herself that she was reading something into nothing. Of course he was tired. They were both tired. Neither of them slept much any more. Because they weren't able to conduct their relationship in daylight, they'd become nocturnal.

'I'm going to have to make a move.' Evanna rose to her feet with difficulty, a hand on her back. 'I never realised how uncomfortable these chairs are.'

Conner drained his glass. 'I don't suppose any chair is comfortable when you're carrying an elephant around in your stomach.'

Evanna laughed good-naturedly and Flora reached for her bag, grateful for the change of subject.

Jim was back with the lads, laughing about something that had happened to the lifeboat crew, and Conner was listening to Logan talking about his plans to extend the surgery.

For now, at least, it appeared that their secret was still safe. Although how long it would take for the locals to realise that she was the girl that Conner was seeing was anyone's guess.

And then what would happen?

Restless and angry with himself, Conner paced the length of his consulting room and back again.

Why had he ever let things go this far?

Buzzing for his first patient, he decided that he had to do

something about the situation. Fast. Before it exploded in his face.

'Dr MacNeil?' Ann Carne stood in the doorway and Conner gave a reluctant laugh.

'If there's one thing I don't need this morning, it's an encounter with my old headmistress.' *And Flora's aunt.*

'I don't see why. Nothing I said ever worried you when you were young,' Ann said crisply, closing the door behind her and making her way to the chair. 'And I don't suppose that's changed just because you've grown up. And, anyway, it seems that no lecture is needed. You've made quite an impression since you returned to Glenmore, Conner.'

'Bad, I'm sure.'

'You know that isn't true.' She looked at him steadily. 'Evidently you're a reformed character. I've come to find out if you're as good a doctor as they say you are.'

Conner sighed. 'Is this like classroom testing?'

'You flew through every exam you ever bothered to take, Conner MacNeil. But while we're on that subject, there's something I want to say, so I may as well get it out of the way before we start.' Ann took a deep breath. 'We didn't help you enough. *I* didn't help you. That's been on my conscience for many years.'

Conner's eyes narrowed. 'I sense that this conversation is about to make both of us extremely uncomfortable so why don't we just skip straight to the part where you tell me your symptoms?'

'In a minute.' Her voice was quiet and Ann shook her head slowly, a hint of sadness in her eyes. 'You were the brightest, most able boy that ever passed through my school, Conner MacNeil.'

'And we both know I passed through it as quickly as I could,' Conner drawled lightly. 'I made a point of not resting my backside on the chair long enough to get bored.'

'You had a brilliant brain, but you were so disruptive and

angry that it took me a long time to see it. Too long. By the time I realised the extent of your abilities it was too late to harness them because you were almost totally wild. You were off the rails, fighting everyone. No one could get through to you. Not the teaching staff. Not your father.' She paused and took a deep breath. 'We didn't know how bad things were for you at home. You covered it up so well. We thought your father was the one struggling with you, not the other way round.'

'I certainly didn't make his life a picnic.'

'He let you down. We all let you down.'

Conner kept his expression neutral. 'This is history and you know I hated history. Science was my subject. I never saw the point of lingering in the past.'

'There's a point when the past is affecting the future.'

'It isn't.'

'Isn't it? Are you married, Conner MacNeil? Are you living with some warm, kind, stable woman who is carrying your child?'

Conner sat for a moment, eye to eye with his old headmistress. 'My marital status has nothing to do with my father.'

'Of course it does. Are you pretending that it didn't affect you? Your wild behaviour was a reaction to everything that was happening at home, I see that now.' She shook her head again. 'I've been teaching for thirty-one years and you were the only child who passed through the doors of my school that I just couldn't cope with. The island couldn't cope with you. We all let you down and for that we owe you an apology.'

'I don't suppose the people whose property I destroyed would agree with you.

'You certainly left your mark on the place. And you're still leaving it, although this time the damage is more subtle.' Ann straightened her shoulders. 'My niece is in love with you. I suppose you know that?'

Conner swore softly and Ann's mouth tightened.

'Behave yourself! Just because you're a grown man, it doesn't mean that I'm prepared to accept that sort of language.'

'What are you going to do? Put me in detention?' Conner gave a short laugh. 'Did she tell you that?'

'No. In fact, I doubt she even knows herself. But I've heard the way she talks about you. Her eyes sparkle and every story that falls from her lips involves something you've done. Every other word she speaks is your name. So what are you going to do about it, Conner?'

Conner rubbed his fingers over his forehead. 'I expect I'll walk out and leave her crying. That's what I usually do.'

'Perhaps.' Ann's tone was calm. 'Or perhaps you'll see sense and realise that a warm, soft, kind woman like Flora is just what you need.'

'It doesn't matter what I need. I do know that whatever *she* needs, it isn't me.'

Ann smiled. 'So you've learned to think about someone other than yourself. That's good, Conner. And don't underestimate Flora. She's shy, not weak. There's more to her than meets the eye.'

Conner's hand dropped. 'So I've discovered.' He thought of Flora half-naked in the sea. Flora turning up at his barn wearing only underwear under her coat. *Flora riding him lightly, her brown curls tumbling over her shoulders.*

Ann was giving him the look she reserved for very naughty students. 'I just thought someone should tell you that you don't have to live up to your reputation. From what I've seen, Bad Conner has a good side. Why not develop it?'

Conner gave a mock shudder. 'That sounds like the lecture you gave me when you told me I should be interested in algebra.' He stirred. 'All right, enough. Is there a medical reason that you're here?'

'I have asthma. Or so they say. Started two years ago, out of nowhere. Completely ridiculous at my age, but there you are. Anyway, Logan started me off on an inhaler, and Dr Walker—

he was your predecessor—gave me another one but they're not working any more.'

'And you say that because…?'

'I'm breathless all the time. Wheezing. Tight chest.' She sighed. 'I tried to walk the cliff path yesterday and had to sit down and look at the view instead. You're going to say that I shouldn't be exercising at my age—'

'Exercise is important at every age.' Conner studied his computer screen and his face broke into a slow smile. 'Well, Miss Carne, I see you were a smoker for fifteen years. I wonder how much money I could make selling that information?'

'I haven't touched one for sixteen years,' she said briskly, 'and everyone has to have a vice.'

'I couldn't agree more. I couldn't survive without my vices.' Conner stood up and took a peak-flow meter out of the drawer. 'Have you been monitoring your own peak flow?'

'Yes. Of course. I'm a teacher. I do everything by the book.' She delved into her bag and pulled out a chart. 'Here.'

He scanned it. 'This shortness of breath—is it just on exercise or when you're doing daily tasks?'

'Exercise. But I can't do as much.'

'And have you had a chest infection? Anything that might have been a trigger?'

He questioned her carefully, listened to the answers and then checked her inhaler technique. 'You should be inhaling slowly and then holding your breath for ten seconds.'

'That's what I'm doing.'

Conner questioned her further and then sat back down and looked at the computer screen. 'You're already taking salbu-tamol and an inhaled steroid. I'm going to add in a long-acting drug and see if that helps. If it does, you can carry on taking it. If it doesn't, we might increase the dose of your inhaled steroid.'

'I'm not wild about taking yet another drug.'

'If your symptoms stabilise, we can reassess in a few months.'

'So I should come back and see you in a few weeks?'

'Yes, or sooner if things don't settle.' He handed her the prescription and she took it with a smile of thanks.

'You've done well with your life, Conner.' She walked towards the door and paused. 'Do the right thing by my niece.'

The right thing.

Conner watched as she left the room and closed the door behind her.

What exactly was the right thing?

The rumours grew from soft whispers to blatant speculation until all the inhabitants of Glenmore had the same question on their lips.

Who was the woman that Conner MacNeil was seeing?

'She lives up your way,' Meg told Flora as she sprinkled chocolate onto a cappuccino. 'People have heard his motorbike roaring down the lanes late at night. Do you want anything to eat with this? Croissant? Chocolate muffin?'

'No, thanks.' Flora handed over the money and took the coffee, just wanting to escape before the conversation could progress any further.

'I mean, who lives near you? Who is likely to catch our Conner's eye? Tilly Andrews? No, it couldn't possibly be her.' Meg frowned as she rang up the amount on the till. 'I just can't imagine.'

'Me neither. Thanks for this, Meg.' Almost stumbling in her haste to make her exit, Flora backed towards the door while Meg pondered.

'I don't see why everyone is so interested anyway. This is Conner we're talking about. He'll have left the island or moved on to the next woman before we've identified the current one.' She wiped the side with some kitchen paper. 'You be careful out there today. There's a storm brewing. Jim reckons it's going to be a big one.'

'Is that right?' Not wanting to think about Conner leaving the island, Flora backed out of the door and took her coffee to the quay, where she sipped it slowly, watching the tourists pick their way off the ferry, most of them a pale shade of green after a rough sea crossing. Beyond them, the sea lashed angrily at the harbour walls and the sky turned ominously dark, despite the fact it was only lunchtime.

Flora sighed. Wild summer storms were a feature of Glenmore but that didn't mean that they welcomed it. If the ferry stopped running then the tourists didn't come, and if the tourists stopped then so did the money that contributed so much to the island economy. They were already in August and the summer months would soon be over.

And then Conner would be gone.

And she'd always known that, hadn't she? She'd always known that his presence on the island was only temporary.

Determined not to think about that, Flora finished her coffee and threw the empty container in the bin. She was not going to ruin the present by worrying about the future.

They still had the rest of summer together.

Climbing into her car, she drove back to the surgery, knowing that she was facing a full clinic now that Evanna had finally stopped work.

She worked through without a break and was just tidying up after her last patient when Conner walked into the room.

As usual her heart jumped and her mood lifted. Just seeing him made her want to smile. 'The weather's awful. There's a strong chance you're going to be trapped indoors tonight, Dr MacNeil.'

'Is that right?'

'Do you fancy being trapped indoors with me?'

'I might.' He pulled her against him and kissed her hungrily.

'As long as you promise to put your book away for half an hour.'

'That depends…' she curled her arms round his neck. '…on whether there is something more exciting to do than read.'

'Is that a challenge?'

'Do you need one?'

His answer was to kiss her again and she sank against him, her body erupting in a storm of excitement. They were lost in each other, absorbed, transported, and neither of them heard the click of the door behind them.

'What the—?' Logan's voice penetrated the fog of excitement that had anaesthetised her brain, and Flora opened her eyes dizzily, trying to remember where she was.

'Logan.' She said his name breathlessly and snatched her hands guiltily away from Conner's chest.

Logan gave a low growl of anger. 'Damn you, Conner, *what the hell do you think you're doing*?'

'Kissing your practice nurse.' Conner's tone was cool, almost bored. But he released his grip on her bottom and shrugged. 'Caught red-handed.' His gaze slid to Flora and he gave a faint smile. 'Or perhaps I should say red-faced.'

Flora froze as Logan turned his disbelieving gaze on her. *'Flora?'*

She stood, trapped in the headlights of his disapproval. *This was it, then.* The moment that had been inevitable.

The moment of discovery.

She waited to feel embarrassed, but nothing happened. Tentatively, she examined the way she felt. Did she want the floor to open up and swallow her? No, she didn't. Did she wish she could turn the clock back? Absolutely not.

Flora frowned slightly, wondering why Logan's incredulous glance had so little effect on her. And then she looked at Conner—at the hard lines of his handsome face—and everything inside her disintegrated. Everything she'd thought she was, *everything she'd thought she wanted*—it all descended into rubble and she realised that the reason she wasn't embarrassed was because she didn't *care* what Logan thought. And the reason she didn't care what Logan thought was because she loved Conner.

She loved him.

Even though it was foolish and she was going to end up in tears, she was completely and utterly crazy about Conner.

She stood for a moment, shocked, exhilarated and absolutely terrified.

Then she turned to Logan, about to tell him that she didn't care what he thought, but something in his expression caught her attention. 'Logan? Is something wrong?'

Logan was glaring at Conner. 'You just can't help it, can you? You have to cause trouble. I ought to punch your lights out.'

'You're right,' Conner drawled, 'you probably should.'

'Stop it, both of you.' Flora was staring at Logan, her concern mounting as she noticed the unnatural pallor of his skin. 'Something has happened, hasn't it? Is it Kirsty? For goodness' sake, say something! You're scaring me.'

'Kirsty's fine.' Logan's voice was harsh. 'But Evanna's waters have broken.'

'Oh…' Flora immediately stepped forward and closed her fingers over his arm, her grip offering reassurance and support. 'It will be fine, Logan. Where is she?'

'In the car. I'm taking her to the ferry.' His breathing unsteady, Logan looked at Conner. 'I just came to tell you that the two of you are in charge. And then you—'

'Forget that,' Flora interrupted him. 'What's happening to Kirsty?'

'Meg is having her, but if she needs any help—'

'That's fine,' Flora said quickly. 'Of course.'

'You're taking Evanna to the ferry?' Conner frowned. 'The last thing I heard, the ferry wasn't going to run. There's a storm brewing, Logan.'

'I know there's a storm. And that's why we're getting off this island while we still can. I've already left it too late. We should have gone last weekend but Evanna is so damn stubborn.'

'But—'

'I know what I'm doing,' Logan said harshly, yanking open the door. 'Just keep an eye on the place while I'm gone.' He glared angrily at Conner. 'And try not to kiss anybody else.'

Janet appeared in the doorway, her face white. 'Logan, you have to come. Evanna says she wants to push. I've helped her out of the car and back into the house.'

'No!' Logan raked a hand through his hair, his voice sharp with panic. 'That isn't right. I don't want Evanna in the house. I want her on the ferry. And if the ferry isn't running, we'll call the air ambulance—'

Flora took control. 'If she wants to push, Conner should take a look at her.'

'I don't want him anywhere near my wife!' Logan rounded on him like a wounded animal and Conner's eyes narrowed.

'Relax. My taste has never run to heavily pregnant women.'

Flora sighed with exasperation and waved Janet away. 'Get me a delivery pack, Janet. Evanna's room. Tall cupboard on the right, top shelf. You two...' She turned to Logan and Conner, her eyes flashing with exasperation. 'Enough. All this testosterone is starting to get on my nerves and I can't concentrate. Logan, listen to me.' Stepping forward, she closed her hand over his wrist, her voice crisp. 'You are in no fit state to assess your wife's progress in labour. Conner and I will do that.' She could feel his pulse thundering under her fingers. 'We'll do that now. If Evanna is going to have this baby imminently, we need to be prepared.'

Conner looked as though he was about to speak and Flora silenced him with a glare, her instincts warning her that he was about to say something Logan didn't need to hear.

'She's not having our baby on this island.' Logan inhaled deeply and looked at her, his eyes bright with fear. *'I am not losing my wife!'*

CHAPTER TEN

'IT WOULD really help if someone could tell me what is going on here,' Conner drawled as he and Flora followed Logan through the surgery to the door that connected with their house. 'My cousin, who I always considered to be of sound mind, appears to have lost the plot. Given that he isn't usually prone to bouts of hysterics, I'm assuming there's a reason.'

Flora paused until Logan was out of earshot. 'He hasn't told you what happened to his first wife?'

'I never asked.'

Flora rolled her eyes. 'Men! OK. Well, to keep it brief, Logan was married before. His first wife died in childbirth, here on Glenmore. There was a terrible storm and he couldn't get her off the island and she...' Flora bit her lip. 'Well, she died. There isn't time to tell you more than that. There was nothing anyone could do, but don't try telling Logan that because he still blames himself.'

'Right.' Conner lifted his eyes and stared at his cousin's retreating shoulders. 'So we can expect him to be very relaxed and calm about the whole thing.'

'If he can't get Evanna off Glenmore for the delivery, he'll probably have a breakdown. We have to be very, very sensitive about this whole situation,' Flora said quietly, and Conner shot her a look, his expression faintly mocking.

'Sensitive? Perhaps I should just leave right now.'

'Don't be ridiculous. We need a plan. You can deliver the baby, I'll reassure Evanna and Logan—'

'No way.' Conner lifted his hands and stopped her in mid flow. 'I don't deliver babies. The only thing I know about babies is how *not* to produce them.'

Flora stared at him. 'Are you telling me you've never delivered a baby before? You're a doctor.'

His gaze was sardonic. 'There isn't a great deal of need for obstetrics in the army. Of course I've delivered a few babies but let's just say that my experience in that area is limited.'

'Mine, too. But we mustn't let them know that.' Flora bit her lip and thought fast. 'It doesn't matter. I can deliver the baby as long as it's straightforward. If there's a problem, you'll have to help. It will be fine. What they really need is reassurance. We just need to be confident. Really confident. Babies come by themselves...' she glanced at him doubtfully '...usually.'

'I can do confident,' Conner said, a trace of humour in his eyes, 'but I can tell you now that Logan isn't going to let me touch his wife.'

'Logan is traumatised. He'll do what we tell him.' She pushed him through the door and he lifted an eyebrow.

'I didn't know you were capable of being so dominating. Don't ever expect me to believe you're shy after this performance.'

Flora shrugged. 'You don't know me at all, do you?'

'Evidently not.'

They found Evanna in the breakfast room, a huge sunny room at the back of the house that adjoined the kitchen and looked over the garden.

'You can't possibly want to push,' Logan was saying in a hoarse voice, his arm round Evanna's shoulders. 'This is your first baby. First babies take ages. Days sometimes.'

Evanna's face was pale and streaked with sweat. 'Not all

first babies take ages.' She broke off and Flora could see that
she was struggling with pain.

Agitated, Logan stood up. 'I'm calling the air ambulance.'

'The wind's too strong,' Conner said in an even tone. 'They
can't fly. I've already rung them.'

Evanna lifted a hand and touched Logan's face. 'You have
to calm down,' she urged softly. 'You're panicking and I need
you.'

'I'm not panicking,' Logan said tightly. 'I'm sorry.'

'Don't be sorry. I understand—and I love you.'

'All right—enough.' Conner pulled a face. 'You're making
me feel ill. Flora, did I hear you asking Janet for a delivery
pack? I presume such a thing exists on this godforsaken
island?'

'We have everything,' Logan growled, his hair roughened
from the number of times he'd run his fingers through it. 'I
made sure. I've got the equipment to do a Caesarean section
if it's necessary.'

'It's not going to be necessary,' Conner said calmly, washing
his hands. 'Evanna, I'm going to take a look and see what's
happening. Logan, go and check on Kirsty.'

Logan's jaw tightened. 'I'm not leaving her.'

Conner inhaled deeply and let the water stream off his hands
into the sink. 'Leave the room, Logan. All this drama is giving
me a headache.'

'No.'

Conner dried his hands and then pulled on the gloves Flora
handed him. 'I can't concentrate with you hovering, ready to
shout abuse at me.'

'What do you know about delivering babies?'

'I'm full of surprises.' Conner turned away from Logan and
concentrated on Evanna, his smile gentle. 'The problem is that
no one on this island trusts me.'

She gave a wan smile. 'I trust you, Conner.'

'It's all going to be fine, you know that, don't you?'

She swallowed. 'Yes…' Her voice faltered but she returned his smile. 'Of course it is. Have you—have you ever delivered a baby before?'

'Do you think I'd be here now if I hadn't? I love delivering babies,' Conner said smoothly, moving to her right side and glancing at Flora, his gaze faintly mocking. 'Delivering babies is my favourite thing.'

Evanna clutched his arm. 'You really have done it before?'

'Loads of times,' Conner said easily, and Logan snorted.

'Oh, for goodness' sake! I suppose you're going to try and convince us that the army is popping out babies all the time.'

'Of course not.' Conner's gaze didn't flicker. 'But the locals are. And they always came to us for help.'

Evanna gave a low moan and reached for Flora's hand. 'Actually, Logan, I think you should ring Meg and check on Kirsty. She was a bit off colour this morning.'

'But—'

'Logan!' Evanna's voice was surprisingly firm. 'You have to let Conner do this. We're wasting time. *I tell you this baby is coming now, whether you like it or not.*'

Flora realised that it was the first time ever she'd heard Evanna raise her voice and Logan took several deep breaths, his face a mask of indecision. 'All right—but I'll be back.' He strode away from them and Conner crouched down beside Evanna.

'Are you comfortable there?'

'I don't think I'd be comfortable anywhere,' she gasped, wincing as another contraction hit her. 'Wait a minute. I can't— Oh, Conner, I want to push—really…'

'Just hold on.' Flora dropped to her knees beside her friend. 'We're going to take a look, see if we can see the baby's head. We need to assess what's happening.'

'I can tell you what's happening,' Evanna muttered, her teeth gritted. 'I'm a midwife. This baby is coming. I think it's called precipitate labour.'

'Well, that's good news,' Conner said lightly. 'If there's one thing I can't stand, it's hanging around.'

Janet hurried into the room with the delivery pack.

'Open it,' Conner ordered brusquely. 'We're both wearing sterile gloves.'

'Open it fast,' Flora said calmly. 'I can see the head. In fact, I'd say it will crown with the next contraction.' *It was too quick*, she thought to herself. *Much too quick.* 'Don't push, Evanna. Can you take some shallow breaths? Pant? That's brilliant. Janet, put the central heating on.'

Janet stared at her. 'It's the middle of the summer.'

'It's not that warm in here and it's stormy outside. The temperature will drop and I want to heat the room a bit. And warm some towels.' *Just in case.*

Evanna groaned. 'I have to push. I can't not push. You have no idea. I've got another contraction coming— I can feel the head, Flora.'

'I know. It's brilliant,' Flora said cheerfully, ignoring Conner's ironic glance. She used her left hand to control the escape of the head and then gently allowed it to extend, remembering the deliveries she'd observed in her training. 'It's all fine, Evanna. The head is out.' *And terrifying.*

'Is he breathing? Is the cord round the neck? It's too fast. Logan was right,' Evanna gasped, tears trickling out of her eyes.

'That's nonsense, Evanna,' Flora said. She gently felt for the cord and her heart plummeted when she felt something. Struggling not to panic, she slid her fingers under it and slipped it over the baby's head. Only then did she start to breathe again. 'Everything is fine, Evanna. And there's nothing wrong with having a baby at home, you know that. You're a midwife!'

Suddenly aware that Conner was right by her side, Flora glanced at him. 'Is someone going to call Logan? He should be here for the next bit.'

'No.' Evanna grabbed his hand. 'It will be too much for him.'

But the decision was taken out of their hands because Logan appeared in the doorway, his face grey. 'Oh, God—what can I do?'

'Pour yourself a whisky and hold Evanna's hand,' Conner advised, and Flora glanced at him.

'Actually, you can draw up the Syntometrine so that Conner can give it.'

Evanna gave another gasp. 'Flora, I've got another one coming.'

'Great.' Flora smiled at her, concentrated on delivering the anterior shoulder and then the baby slithered out, red-faced and bawling. 'Little boy. Congratulations.' She lifted the wriggling bundle onto Evanna's abdomen and covered him with the warmed towels that Janet quietly handed her.

'Oh, Logan…' Tears spilled down Evanna's cheeks as she curved her arm protectively around the baby.

Logan stared down at his wife and son, his eyes bright. He didn't speak. Then he lifted a hand and pressed his fingers to his eyes, clearly struggling for control.

Conner rose to his feet. 'She's fine,' he said softly. 'They're both fine. Your family is safe. You can relax.' He hesitated for a moment and then reached out a hand and closed his fingers over his cousin's shoulder. Flora felt a lump build in her own throat as she saw the gesture of support and reassurance.

Who said Conner wasn't capable of forming relationships?

Who said that he wasn't capable of feeling?

Knowing that her work wasn't finished, Flora turned her attention back to the delivery. She clamped the cord twice, divided it and then attached a Hollister clamp near the umbilicus. 'Two normal arteries, Evanna,' she murmured. 'Everything is looking good here.' She gently applied traction to the cord and the placenta slid out into the bowl.

'I'll check it.' Logan stepped forward to help, his face regaining some of its colour. 'I'm feeling fine now. Thank you. Both of you.'

'He's already feeding, Logan.' Evanna sounded sleepy and delighted at the same time. 'What are we going to call him?'

They murmured together and Flora's eyes misted as she watched them with their new son. Logan's hands were gentle, his face softened by love, and Evanna looked as though she'd won the lottery.

Feeling a lump in her throat, Flora glanced towards Conner. He was standing at the French windows, staring out across the garden, his shoulders tense and his features frozen.

She wondered what he was thinking.

Was he remembering his own family, and the contrast they must have made to the scene playing out in front of him?

They'd shared enough secrets in the stillness of the night for her to know that he would be less than comfortable with such undiluted domesticity.

Wanting to help, she stood up and swiftly cleared everything away. 'We're going to leave the two of you alone for a few minutes,' she said to Logan. 'We'll be next door if you need us.' She washed her hands quickly and then touched Conner's arm.

He turned, his face expressionless. 'Yes?'

'I don't think we're needed here.' She gestured with her head. 'Let's go next door.'

'Sure.' With a faint shrug he followed her through to the surgery and they walked into her room. But he didn't reach for her or make any of his usual wry, disparaging comments. Instead, he seemed distant. Remote. 'So—I didn't know you were a midwife.'

'I'm not. That's the first baby I've ever delivered.'

Conner gave a short laugh. 'You're full of surprises. I never would have known.'

'Do you want to know the truth? I was always terrified that this baby would come when Evanna was on the island and I knew Logan would panic. So I read a few books, asked Evanna a few questions...' Flora shrugged, wishing that he'd relax with her. 'I had a nasty moment when I felt the cord but it was all fine. And it helped knowing you were there.'

'I was as much use as a hog roast at a vegetarian supper,' he drawled. 'You did it all.'

'That's not true. You were strong,' she said softly. 'You gave Evanna confidence, and if something had happened to her or the baby, you would have known what to do. You're good in an emergency.'

He looked at her for a moment and then looked away. 'Well, they're both all right, and that's all that matters.' He glanced at his watch. 'I'd better get going, or Logan will be grumbling that I haven't finished my paperwork.'

Flora felt a flicker of desperation.

Something had changed between them and she didn't know what it was.

She wanted to say something about Logan and Evanna. She wanted to show him that she understood how hard it must be for him, but he was cool and remote, discouraging any sort of personal intrusion into his thoughts or feelings. And, anyway, she didn't want to have that conversation here, where they could be interrupted at any moment. 'Are you busy tonight?'

'Why do you ask?'

Her heart skipped. 'Because I thought you might fancy skinny-dipping in the sea. It's a great form of relaxation.'

He stood for a moment and then he turned. His ice-blue eyes were serious and there was no hint of a smile on his mouth. 'I don't think so.'

Her heart plummeted. 'I'll take off my bra and knickers this time, if that would swing your decision.'

'No, Flora.' His voice held none of its usual mockery. 'I don't think that's a good idea.'

'Oh. I thought you— I thought we might—' She broke off, not knowing what to say. 'Of course. Sorry. I understand.'

Had he guessed how she felt about him?

Probably. Sooner or later it happened to every woman who spent time with him, she was sure of that.

He'd guessed, and now he was running for cover. She'd always known this moment would come, but that didn't make it any easier. In fact, the pain was so overwhelming that she turned away, not wanting to embarrass herself or him by saying anything else.

'This thing between us has to end, Flora. *Do you understand?*' He closed his hands around her upper arms and spun her towards him, his eyes fierce as he stared into her face. 'Do you?'

Even though she'd sensed this moment was coming, she felt totally unprepared. 'Yes,' she croaked. 'I understand, Conner.' If he didn't want to be with her, she couldn't change that. And she didn't want to make him feel bad by showing how much she was hurting. 'We've been together for over a month.' She gave a tremulous smile. 'That's probably a record for you. Don't feel guilty. We had a great time. I had a great time.'

He gritted his teeth. 'Don't cry.'

'I'm not going to cry.' *At least, not until she was on her own.*

And she wasn't going to admit that she loved him either, because that would just make the whole situation even more embarrassing for both of them.

And what was the point of it?

His fingers tightened on her arms. 'We never should have started this,' he said hoarsely. '*I* never should have started it.'

'You didn't. I did. And, Conner, you're hurting me.'

'Sorry.' He released her instantly and let out a breath. 'Sorry.'

'You don't have to look so tormented.' Though it took all her courage, she was determined to say it. 'You never promised me anything. You haven't done anything wrong. It was just a bit of fun.'

'And will it be fun when the locals work out who the woman

is that I've been seeing? No, it won't.' His tone impatient and full of self-loathing, he turned away from her and strode towards the window. 'I can't believe I thought for a moment we could have a secret affair on an island like Glenmore. I'd forgotten what the place was like. You can't sneeze without someone counting the microbes.'

'I didn't think you cared what people say about you.'

'I don't. But I care about what people say about *you*. I saw your face, Flora,' he said roughly, 'when you were looking at that baby. You watched Evanna and Logan and you wanted what they have. Admit it.'

'I admit it,' she said simply. 'Who wouldn't want that, Logan? Someone to love. A family. Isn't it what everyone wants?'

His hands dropped to his sides. 'I can't do this. I'm sorry, Flora.'

'Is this because of Evanna and Logan?' Suddenly she couldn't just let him walk away. 'Talk to me, Conner. I know you're upset about what just happened and I can imagine it must be very hard seeing all that family stuff when your own family life was so desperately bad, but—'

He jerked away from her and strode towards the door. 'Enough.'

'Please, talk to me, Conner. I can see you're upset. Come over later. Even if we don't...' She stumbled over the words. 'If we're not still together, I'm still your friend. '

He paused with his hand on the door and then he turned slowly. And then he looked at her and his eyes were bleak and empty. 'People are already talking.'

'I know.'

'They're going to find out, Flora,' he said roughly. 'Nods. Winks. Whispers. Everyone wondering what a girl like you is doing with a man like me. And you'll hate it. You hate being the focus of attention. Take that first night—you were mortified when Jim and the others turned up on the beach.'

'Well of course I was.' She defended herself. 'I was in my underwear!'

'It was more than that. You didn't want people gossiping about you. And the whispers have started all over Glenmore. Do you think I haven't heard them? In the pub the other night, you almost cracked your glass because you were so terrified that Jim had discovered just who I'd been visiting in the dead of night. Knowing this place, people are grilling you every time you go to buy eggs or milk. Am I right?'

'Yes, but—'

'And you'll hate that because you're so shy. And I don't want people breathing your name and mine in the same sentence.' His knuckles whitened on the doorhandle. 'You know what people say about me. I'm bad Conner. People expect me to go the same way my father went.'

'I keep telling you that you are *not* your father.'

'No, but you deserve to be with a man you're not ashamed to be seen with.'

'I'm not ashamed of what we share, Conner.'

'Yes, you are, because you're not the sort of woman to indulge in wild affairs, especially not with men like me. When Logan walked in and caught us kissing, you jumped like a kangaroo on a hot plate and your cheeks were the colour of strawberries.'

'Well, of course! But that wasn't about you, it was about me. I'm not used to...' she shrugged self-consciously '...kissing and stuff in public.'

'And you're not going to get used to it. I have no intention of dragging your reputation down into the dirt. You have to live here after I've left.' He took her face in his hands and looked at her. 'So far the only person who knows is Logan and he won't say anything. Our secret should be safe.'

Confused, she shook her head. 'Is that why you're ending it? Because of what people might think of me?'

'Look me in the eye and tell me you haven't spent years

dreaming about finding the right man, about having babies and being a family here on Glenmore.'

Incurably truthful, Flora nodded. 'I have imagined that, of course, but—'

'Of course you have. And you deserve that. You'll be a great mother.' With a faint smile he lifted her hand to his lips in an old-fashioned gesture and then cursed softly and dragged her against him. 'Sorry, but I think I'm going to be bad one more time.' He lowered his mouth to hers and kissed her slowly and thoroughly until her heart was hammering and her legs were weak. Then he lifted his head and smiled. 'Now, go away and find a man who is going to make you happy.'

Without giving her a chance to reply, he turned and left the room, leaving her staring after him with a head full of questions and a heart full of misery.

'Conner is in such a foul mood,' Evanna murmured, tucking the baby expertly onto her shoulder and rubbing his back. 'The rumour is that whoever he was seeing has dumped him. I told Meg that's *completely* ridiculous because when in this lifetime did a woman ever dump Conner? Flora, are you listening to a word I'm saying?'

'Yes. No.' Flora lifted her fingers to her throbbing head. 'Sorry—I didn't really hear you. What did you say?'

Three days had passed since Conner had ended their relationship. Three days in which she hadn't eaten or slept. She felt as though part of her had been ripped out.

'I was just talking about Conner.' Evanna frowned. 'I can't believe a woman has dumped him because what woman in their right mind would dump him? On the other hand, I haven't seen any broken-hearted women around the place. Everyone is behaving as they usually behave. What's the matter with you? Why are you rubbing your head?'

'Bad night.' Flora curved her mouth into something that she hoped resembled a smile. 'Too much on my mind.'

She missed him so much.

She missed sleeping in his arms, she missed their long, intimate conversations in the darkness of the night, and she missed the way he made love.

He'd ended it because he thought she wanted to get married and have children. Or had he ended it because he was afraid that the ever-increasing rumours would hurt her? She wasn't sure any more. She'd replayed their last conversation in her head so many times that she felt as though her brain had turned into spaghetti.

Evanna looked guilty. 'It's our fault. Logan and I are so wrapped up in little Charlie and you and Conner are working so hard covering for the pair of us. How has he been with you? Moody?'

'I don't see that much of him. We do our own clinics.' Flora stood up quickly. 'Great to see you and Charlie looks great, too, and—'

'Flora…' Evanna peered closely at her. 'What is the matter with you? You're behaving very oddly. Is it the baby?' Her voice softened. 'Has it made you all broody? I know how much you want your own family and it *will* happen. One day you're going to meet the man of your dreams and have a family of your own.'

'Yes.' Flora felt as though her face was going to crack. 'Absolutely.' And she realised that her dream didn't seem so clear any more.

What she wanted was to be with Conner.

And if he didn't want to get married or have a family—well, she'd live with that.

But he didn't want *her*, did he?

He'd ended the relationship.

Evanna's hand stilled on the baby's back. 'I wish you'd tell me what's wrong.' She frowned. 'Flora?'

Flora looked at Evanna and Charlie. And she thought of Logan and what they shared.

And then she thought of what she'd had with Conner.

Had he at any point actually said that he didn't want her? No. Yet again she ran through the conversation in her head, trying to remember every last detail. What he'd said was that he wasn't the right man for her. That she wouldn't want to be seen with him in public.

And when he'd said that, she hadn't argued with him because, as usual, she hadn't known what to say. She'd let him walk away because she hadn't thought of the right thing to say at the right time.

But suddenly she knew exactly what she wanted to say.

Maybe he didn't want her any more, but she needed to find out. And she didn't care about pride because some things were more important than pride.

Panic fluttered inside her. 'Evanna, where is Conner, do you know?'

'He went to the Stag's Head for a drink with Logan.'

Flora glanced at the clock on the wall. Seven o'clock. The chances were that most of Glenmore would be in the Stag's Head at this hour on a Friday night. She stood up. 'I'm really sorry to abandon you, but I'm going for a drink. There's something I need to say to Conner.'

The Stag's Head was crowded with locals and heads turned as Flora opened the door and paused, her eyes scanning the room.

'Hey, Flora.' Ben smiled at her from behind the bar. 'You look like a woman in need of a drink. What can I get you?'

'In a minute, Ben, thanks.' Finally she spotted Conner and just at that moment he lifted his eyes and saw her. Ice-blue melded with brown and for a moment she just stood still, her heart pounding and her cheeks flaming red, unable to look away or move.

'Hi, Flora,' a couple of the locals called out to her, and she gave a vague smile but didn't respond.

If she didn't do this right away, she'd lose her nerve.

She let the door close behind her and wove her way through the chattering throng towards his table.

His eyes narrowed, but his gaze didn't shift from hers and from behind her came the sound of wolf whistles and good-natured laughter.

'Hey, Conner, looks like our Flora's got something to say to you.'

'Have you been a naughty boy, Con?'

The cat calls and teasing continued and Flora stopped next to him, realising with a flash of desperation that her plan was never going to work. She *did* have something to say, but the pub was so noisy that no one was ever going to hear her. *And she needed them to hear.*

'Flora?' Conner's voice was wary and for a moment she just looked at him, wondering how she was going to do this.

She opened her mouth to speak and then closed it again, thinking rapidly.

Executing a rapid change of plan, she leaned forward, took his face in her hands and kissed him. He stiffened with shock and his mouth remained immobile under hers. Then he started to pull away from her, so she slid onto his lap, straddling him, her hands clasping his head, keeping his mouth against hers.

A stunned silence had descended on the pub and although she didn't turn her head to look, Flora knew that everyone was staring at them. And that was hardly surprising because she was creating the biggest spectacle that Glenmore had seen for a long time. Which had been her intention.

Despite the tension in his body, she felt Conner's mouth move under hers and then felt the skilled stroke of his tongue. It was as if he couldn't help himself and, as always, the chemistry flashed between them. But his lapse was short-lived and this time when he pulled away he removed her hands at the same time, clasping her wrists firmly.

He stared at her, his blue eyes blazing. *'What do you think you're doing?'*

The noise around them had ceased. The low hum of chatter had died, the laughter was silenced and there was no clink of glasses.

'I'm kissing you, Conner,' Flora said clearly. 'I'm kissing you, just as I've kissed you every day for the past month. Only this time I'm doing it in public, so there's no confusion about the facts.'

His mouth tightened and he muttered something under his breath, but she covered his lips with her fingers.

'No. You had your say the other night. Now it's my turn to talk,' she said calmly, and then she slid off his lap and turned to face everyone. And for a moment her courage faltered because what seemed like a million faces were staring at her.

Her gaze slid over the crowd.

She saw Nick and, behind him, Meg. She saw Janet and Jim. It seemed that everyone was in the Stag's Head.

'You've all been wondering who Conner has been seeing for the last month. Well, it's me,' she said simply, speaking clearly and raising her voice slightly so that everyone could hear her. 'I'm the lucky woman.'

'Flora, for crying out loud.' Conner rose to his feet, dislodging her arm from his shoulder. 'Have you been drinking?'

'No. I'm completely sober.' She smiled up at him, aware that everything she felt shone in her eyes. Then she took his hand and turned back to face the islanders—the people she spent her life with. 'I know what you're all thinking. You're thinking that Bad Conner has lived up to his name again, that obviously he seduced good, sensible Flora because she'd never do anything as reckless as have a wild, passionate affair with a man who is obviously going to walk off into the sunset, leaving her broken-hearted and very possibly pregnant.'

The locals were too shocked to respond so Flora just ploughed on.

'You're wrong. *I* seduced *him*. And I'm not embarrassed about that because I've discovered that—' She broke off as the door to the pub opened and Evanna walked in, holding the baby.

'Charlie and I suddenly had a horrible feeling that we were missing something important so I called a babysitter for Kirsty.'

As if emerging from a trance, Logan rose to his feet and walked over to his wife. He took the baby from her and tipped one of the lifeboat crew out of his chair so that she could sit down.

Flora smiled at her friend. 'Good timing. I was just about to tell everyone that I've discovered that I don't really want what I thought I wanted. Up until a month ago I thought I wanted a man who loved me, a home, children—all the usual things. And then Conner came back.'

Conner's eyes were on hers and he shook his head. 'Stop now, before you make things worse.'

'Things can't get any worse for me, Conner.' Flora touched his cheek gently. 'I've discovered that not being with you is the worst it can get. You're all I want.' She was speaking just to him now, suddenly oblivious to her audience who stood watching, paralysed with surprise and fascination. 'You're all I want, Conner MacNeil. And I want you as you are, for as long as you want to be with me. I know you don't want babies or a family. I know you don't want anything permanent. And that's all right. If all we ever share is hot sex, that's fine.'

Someone in the crowd gulped and she wasn't sure whether the shocked sound had come from Meg or Evanna because she wasn't paying attention.

She was watching Conner.

'I love you,' she said, her eyes misting as she looked at him. 'And I know that probably scares you. I don't think anyone has ever loved you properly before and I want you to know how I feel. And I know you don't feel the same way about me and that's fine. I understand. If I'd been as badly hurt as you were as a child, I wouldn't risk my heart either. But I'm giving you mine, Conner, for as long as you want it. And I'm telling you that in public so that there's no mistake about it. I love you so much. And I'm not ashamed of that. I don't care who knows because I'm proud of what you've become and I'm proud that I'm the one you've spent time with since you've been on Glenmore. And if turns out that you've had enough of me, I'll accept it.' She shrugged. 'But I won't accept you ending our relationship because you're worried about what people might think of me. I don't care what anyone thinks. I just care about you. Us.' She stopped and Logan cleared his throat.

'That's got to be the longest speech you've ever made, Flora Harris.'

Conner stared at her, his face unusually pale. But he didn't speak.

Flora looked at him expectantly. 'Aren't you going to say something? You're the one who's slick with words, Conner MacNeil, not me. You always know what to say.'

Still he didn't answer her. It was as if he'd been turned to stone and she gave a sigh of frustration.

'Did you hear what I said? I'm in love with you.' On impulse, she pulled out a chair, stood on it and turned to face the crowd. 'Flora Harris loves Conner MacNeil!'

Ben cleared his throat and scratched his head. 'We heard you the first time, Flora. We're waiting to hear what Conner has to say. But apparently he's been struck dumb.'

Finally Conner moved. He rose slowly to his feet, gently lifted Flora off the chair and lowered her to the floor as if she were made of porcelain. 'I thought you were shy.'

'I am shy.'

He stroked a strand of hair away from her eyes with a gentle hand. 'I've got news for you, angel. Shy girls don't stand on chairs in pubs and declare undying love.'

'They do if they mean it,' she said softly, and his hand dropped to his side.

'There are things I need to say to you.'

Her heart fluttered. Rejection? Or a stay of execution? 'Then say them.'

'Not here.' He glanced at their audience. 'I think you've had enough of a show for one night.' And then he closed his hand over hers and led her from the pub and out into the darkness.

'Where are we going?' Flora hurried to keep up with him but he didn't answer and eventually they reached the quay where her boat was moored. 'You want to go sailing in the dark?'

'No, but I want to sit and look at her for a minute. Boats always calm me.' He sat down on the edge of the quay and tugged at her hand. 'Sit down.'

She sat, her heart pumping, the surface of the quay rough beneath her legs. 'Are you angry?'

'How could I possibly be angry?' He gave a short laugh, his eyes on the boats. 'I'm not angry. But I can't accept what you're offering, Flora.'

'I love you, Conner. Nothing you do or say is going to change that fact.'

'You don't really want an affair. It isn't who you are.'

'I want *you*. And if an affair is what's on offer then that's what I'll take.' She hesitated and then put her hand on his thigh and left it there. 'There's no pressure on you, Conner. I know you were more than a little spooked by seeing Logan and Evanna. I know that family life isn't what you want—'

'You're wrong.' His voice was hoarse and he covered her hand with his and then gripped it tightly. 'I was spooked, that's true, but I was spooked because in my mind I kept seeing *you* sitting there, holding a baby. And I wanted that baby to be mine.'

His words were so unexpected that for a moment she assumed she must have imagined them. She stared blankly at the boat, afraid to breathe, move or do anything that might disturb the atmosphere. *Afraid to look at him.*

Then, finally, she dared to turn her head. 'What did you say?'

'You heard me.'

Stunned, Flora could do nothing but stare. 'I don't understand.'

'Neither do I. I've spent my entire life running from relationships. I've never given anyone the opportunity to hurt me. But you crept up on me, Flora Harris.' He gave a lopsided smile. 'Somehow you sneaked in under my radar. With you, I didn't feel angry any more. You're the only person I've ever met whose company I prefer to my own.'

She could hardly breathe. 'But if you felt like that, why didn't you tell me? Why did you end our relationship? *Why did you walk away?*'

'Because I'm not a good catch.' He lifted her hand to his lips and kissed it. 'As far as commitment goes, my track record is appallingly bad. What woman in her right mind would take a chance on me?'

'I would,' Flora said softly. 'I would, if you asked me to.'

He was silent for a moment and when he spoke his voice was husky. 'You would? You're not worried about my past?'

'I'm more worried about my future. I can't imagine what it will be like if you're not part of it.'

'Knowing who I am doesn't make a difference?'

'I love who you are,' she said simply. 'You're a man who has done tremendous things with his life, despite the most appalling start. Most people would have crumpled. Most people would have repeated the pattern they'd seen at home or allowed the past to dictate their present. You did neither of those things. You trained as a doctor. You give to others, even though you were given so little yourself.'

He was silent for a moment and then he cleared his throat

and gave her a wry smile. 'Now, this is the sort of hero-worship I think I could live with,' he drawled softly, standing up and pulling her up after him. 'I'm still afraid you're going to lose your nerve any minute and change your mind.'

'I won't do that. I love you, Conner. What I feel for you isn't something I can turn on and off.'

'I make women miserable, Flora.'

'You don't make *me* miserable. These last weeks has been the happiest of my life.'

He hesitated. 'What would you say if I told you that I don't want to stay on Glenmore?'

She lifted a hand to his face, gently exploring the roughness of his jaw with her finger. 'I'd say that's fine. And I'd ask you where you want to go.'

His gaze flickered from her face to the boat. 'I want to sail. Just the two of us. And when you're too pregnant to move around the boat, we'll find some dry land and make a home.'

She felt the lump building in her throat. 'That sounds good to me.'

'You don't mind leaving Glenmore?'

'I want to be wherever you are.'

He closed his eyes for a moment and then lowered his head so that his forehead brushed hers. 'If you'll do this, *if you'll trust me with your heart,* I swear I won't let you down, angel.'

'I know you won't let me down.'

His breath warmed her mouth. 'I don't deserve you. You're such a good person.'

'Actually, you're wrong about that. I have an *extremely* bad side,' she murmured, giving a soft gasp as his lips brushed the corner of her mouth. 'Several less-than-desirable qualities, in fact.'

'Name a few.' His body was pressed against hers and it was becoming harder and harder to concentrate.

'I'm useless at gossip.'

'That's a quality.'

'I'm insatiable in the bedroom.' She tilted her head back and gave him a wicked smile. 'The problem with good girls, Conner MacNeil, is that when they discover what fun being bad can be, they never want to stop.'

'Is that right?' He curved his hands over her bottom and brought his mouth down on hers. And then he suddenly lifted his head and cursed softly.

'What's the matter?'

'What does a person have to do to get privacy on this island?' He stared over her shoulder and Flora turned to find what appeared to be the entire population of Glenmore gathered on the quay, watching.

Several of them held torches and Flora blinked as the beam from one almost blinded her.

'Well?' It was Jim who spoke and his voice carried the short distance across the quay. 'You can't expect to make a declaration like that in the Stag's Head and not tell us the ending. What's the ending? Has she said yes?'

Conner shook his head in disbelief. 'I can't believe this,' he muttered. 'The first and only time I propose to a woman and I have to do it with an audience.'

'You should be down on one knee, Conner MacNeil,' Ann Carne said primly, appearing at the front of the crowd, and Flora's heart stumbled in her chest.

'You don't have to propose—I don't want you to feel smothered by all this. We can just live together and—'

He put a finger over her lips, his eyes gentle. 'That isn't what I want. I want to make sure you're chained to me so that you can't run off easily when you realise what you've married.' He dropped to one knee and she gave an appalled gasp.

'Conner! You don't have to go that far! The seagulls are usually pretty busy above here. Kneeling could be a messy experience.'

'If I don't kneel, I'll never hear the last of it from the locals.'

With an exaggerated gesture Conner took her hand in his. His eyes gleamed wickedly and he lifted an eyebrow in question. 'Well? How daring are you feeling? Can you bring yourself to marry a reprobate like me?'

'Conner!' There was a disgusted snort from Evanna. 'You're *supposed* to make it romantic. At the very least you're supposed to tell her that you love her.'

'I'm on my knees in seagull droppings,' Conner growled. 'I think that tells her quite a lot about my feelings.'

Half laughing, half crying, Flora looked down at him. 'You haven't said that you love me. I want to hear you say it. That's the really important bit.'

'I love you.' This time his voice was serious. 'I love you, Flora Mary Harris. Will you marry me?'

'Yes. Oh, yes. *Yes!*' She choked on the word and tears spilled down her cheeks.

Instantly Conner was on his feet, his expression horrified as he scooped her face into his hands. 'What's wrong?' He brushed the tears away with his thumbs. 'All my life I've been making women cry because I wouldn't say those words. Now, suddenly, I've said them and you're crying!'

'I'm crying because I'm happy.' She pressed her mouth to his. 'I'm happy and I love you. And, just for the record, my answer is yes.'

Torchlight wavered on her face. 'Speak up, Flora! We can't hear you at the back!'

Flora started to laugh. 'Yes,' she yelled in a voice so loud that Conner flinched. *'Yes, I will marry you.'*

There was a cheer from the crowd on the quay and Conner folded her into his arms. 'I hope you know what you're saying yes to, because you can't back out now.'

'I'm saying yes to everything,' Flora said softly, and this time her words were for him alone. 'Everything, Conner.'

'Everything?' His eyes held a wicked gleam. 'In that case,

I don't know about you,' he murmured against her mouth, 'but I think I could do with a bit more privacy for the rest of this conversation. Your place or mine?'

Medical Romance™

COMING NEXT MONTH
TO MEDICAL ROMANCE SUBSCRIBERS

Visit www.eHarlequin.com for more details.

A PROPOSAL WORTH WAITING FOR by Lilian Darcy
Crocodile Creek 24-Hour Rescue
Surgeon Nick Devlin knows he's neglected his son, but going with him to Crocodile Creek Kids' Camp will change that. Nick is the last person Miranda expects to see there—their one passionate night at medical school left her with heartache, and she's determined to keep her distance....

THE SPANISH DOCTOR'S LOVE-CHILD by Kate Hardy
Mediterranean Doctors
Career-driven doctor Leandro Herrera never becomes emotionally involved with women. But then he discovers his new nurse is Becky Marston—the woman he spent one passionate night with.... And Becky announces she's pregnant! Suddenly the hot-blooded Spanish doctor wants the mother of his child as his wife!

A DOCTOR, A NURSE: A LITTLE MIRACLE by Carol Marinelli
Nurse Molly Jones has discovered that pediatrician Luke Williams is back—with four-year-old twins! Single dad Luke is charming—but Molly's heart was broken when Luke left, and when she discovered that, for her, motherhood was never meant to be.

TOP-NOTCH SURGEON, PREGNANT NURSE by Amy Andrews
Nursing manager Beth Rogers forgot her past for one amazing night, not expecting to see her English lover again. He turns out to be hotshot surgeon Gabe Fallon and they'll be working together to save two tiny girls! Then Beth discovers she's carrying his baby.

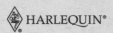

Silhouette

Desire

Gifts from a Billionaire

JOAN HOHL

THE M.D.'S MISTRESS

Dr. Rebecca Jameson collapses from
exhaustion while working at a remote
African hospital. Fellow doctor Seth Andrews
ships her back to America so she can heal.
Rebecca is finally with the sexy surgeon
she's always loved. But would their affair
last longer than the week?

**Available September
wherever books are sold.**

Always Powerful, Passionate and Provocative.

SD76892

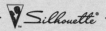

SPECIAL EDITION™

NEW YORK TIMES BESTSELLING AUTHOR

DIANA PALMER

A brand-new Long, Tall Texans novel

HEART OF STONE

Feeling unwanted and unloved, Keely returns
to Jacobsville and to Boone Sinclair, a rancher
troubled by his own past. Boone has always
seemed reserved, but now Keely discovers a
sensuality with him that quickly turns to love. Can
they each see past their own scars to let love in?

*Available September 2008
wherever you buy books.*

Silhouette®

Romantic
SUSPENSE

Sparked by Danger, Fueled by Passion.

The Coltons Are Back!

Marie Ferrarella
Colton's Secret Service

The Coltons: Family First

On a mission to protect a senator, Secret Service agent
Nick Sheffield tracks down a threatening message only
to discover Georgie Gradie Colton, a rodeo-riding single
mom, who insists on her innocence. Nick is instantly
taken with the feisty redhead, but vows not to let his
feelings interfere with his mission. Now he must figure
out if this woman is conning him or if he can trust her
and the passion they share....

Available September wherever books are sold.

**Look for upcoming Colton titles
from Silhouette Romantic Suspense:**

Visit Silhouette Books at www.eHarlequin.com   SRS27598

Thoroughbred Legacy

The purse is set and the stakes are high…

Romance, scandal and glamour set in the exhilarating world of horse racing!

Follow the 12-book continuity, in September with:

Millions to Spare
by BARBARA DUNLOP
Book #5

Courting Disaster
by KATHLEEN O'REILLY
Book #6

Who's Cheatin' Who?
by MAGGIE PRICE
Book #7

A Lady's Luck
by KEN CASPER
Book #8

Available wherever books are sold, including most bookstores, supermarkets, discount stores and drugstores.

www.eHarlequin.com

RCTL0908